SHADOW OF OMEGA
BOOK 2: THE DREAM CORPORATION TRILOGY

SHADOW OF OMEGA

First edition. October 5, 2023.

ISBN: 979-8224230907

Written by Michael TT Williams.

About the Author

MICHAEL TT WILLIAMS was born in South London, United Kingdom. He is a full-time author who specializes in science fiction and fantasy, but also writes other fiction, and non-fiction.

He has lived and worked in several Countries and travelled extensively in more than one hundred more. He has managed a wide number of diverse businesses including in Africa. He holds post-graduate degrees in economics and law and is a sociologist and historian.

He is passionate about animals, music and film, and promoting compassion for all living things.

Books by Michael TT Williams:-
The Dream Corporation Trilogy:
Dark Forces
Shadow of Omega
Reality Rebooted

Other fiction
Donna. A Dream Corporation Chronicle
What the Devil!
Tales from Two Square Metres
The Miner
#1 Bestseller: Star Trek, James T Kirk
The Man who lived Backwards

Non-fiction
The Happiness Index
Our Future with the Virus
Turned Upside Down

Unbelievable True Stories
The small Bodyguard
Young Nero

Acknowledgements

WITH SINCERE THANKS to Fiona and Howard for all their patience, guidance, and help, in the production of this book, and well beyond.

Principles in quantum physics:

At the quantum level, when two waves are laid on top of each other they can momentarily cancel each other out or strengthen each other where they intersect. With a nearly infinite number of waves, the strength is incalculable.

Author's Note

This is a continuation of the Dream Corporation Trilogy which began with "Book 1: "Dark Forces".

THE HUMAN EXPERIENCE is engineered by energy waves, but we live a story.

This is not a horror story, but it *is* part chiller, and a thriller. Although this book moves along traditional lines in many ways, it also breaks with tradition in some key areas. Rather than having a central character featured everywhere, it follows the journeys of several lead characters, men and women, as they weave through dream-worlds, and what we believe is the real world. Although, it might seem, initially, that the characters and their stories are not connected directly, in fact, they are, and this connection is pivotal to the story. A list of characters is provided.

Another way in which this book is not entirely traditional is that it includes technologies that, although predicted, have not yet been invented. Accordingly, in addition to the explanations given in the course of the narrative, a glossary is provided for ease of reference.

Further, since the subject matter of the book rests on a mattress of dreams, the reader will journey through a variety of landscapes, and seemingly different timelines. At times, it will seem surreal; that is, after all, the nature of dreams. And if the reader's experience is sometimes similar to that of being in a dream, then that was precisely the intention. But nothing in this book is impossible or even implausible. The background intention was to encourage all of us to think about our lives and our dreams, and to relish what unites us, rather than what we allow to divide us. It behoves us to treasure what we have, while it lasts, and to share our dreams with open hearts and minds. Otherwise, we squander the time we have, pursuing the pointless, and trying to answer the time worn question: What is the point?

LEAD CHARACTERS

Tarot: Genius inventor of the technology that allows "dreaming."
Karen: Girlfriend/wife of Tarot
Mark: Dreamer looking for Vanessa
Freddy: A Seeker, and guardian to Millie
Millie: Freddy's ward
Donna : Friend to Millie
Geoff: Technician at Dreamcorp
Gladstone: Chief Operations Officer, Dreamcorp
Vanessa & Rio: Twin blondes with Ultra-wave minds
Martin: African citizen of Dystopia, and friend of Rio
Roy: Millie's lost Irish father

Rhea: Gypsy girl in appearance, but, in fact, the artificial intelligence that runs the entire dream-world architecture.

Lucia: Daughter of Varus, Emperor of Rome (Regent)
Lucius Twin brother of Lucia
Marcellus: Vanessa's friend, Lucius' lover
Clovis Leader of the Jeebers in Dystopia
Muna: White Tigress, Tarot's first AI creation
Yusi and Lenta: Twin brothers at Castle Vlad, sons of the Count

GLOSSARY

Dreamer:- A person who is dreaming within the architecture

Architecture:- The system run by artificial intelligence that enables people to control their own dreams.

Figs:- Figments of our imaginations that manifest as characters in dreams.

Seeker:- A private detective who seeks out dreamers, lost, or trapped, in their own dreams

Dream-ware:- Software in the bloodstream that links the unconscious mind with the architecture.

Dream-world:- The environment in which dreams take place

Dream-path:- The path a person takes in a dream, and the most defined part of the dream-scape.

Dream-scape:- The immediate area surrounding the dreamer who is generating the dream.

Random-elasticity:- Describes how time and places expand and contract in the course of a dream.

Bringing up:- Waking up a dreamer without their consent.

Going dark:- When safeguards fail, and dreams pose a danger to dreamers.

Ultra-waves:- The smallest and most powerful waves in creation

Alpha-waves:- Brain waves associated with high intelligence

Theta-waves:- Brain waves associated with dreaming and meditation

The mind:- Distinct from the brain, comprised of waves that are responsible for consciousness, but not understood, except by Tarot

P.s.i.:- Denoting the strength of will-power within the dream architecture

In Dark Forces: Part 1, The Dream Corporation

TAROT WANTS TO CHANGE the world for the better. He founds a company that becomes "The Dream Corporation", a monopoly provider of equipment and services that facilitates "dreaming". Tarot's guiding premise was to create an opportunity for people to be happy and fulfilled in their lives, while they are sleeping, in a manner which is impossible while they are awake.

But after two years, things start going wrong. Mark Moore gets trapped in his dream and a professional Seeker, Freddy Fox, is sent after him. More people are lost in dreams including Millie; and the twins, Vanessa and Rio.

Evidence starts to emerge of a consciousness that is turning dreams dark, and causing comas. Is it alien? Is it malicious Artificial Intelligence, or has the dark side of human nature been uploaded into the system? Donna claims to have been contacted, whilst in a short coma, by entities called "The Architects". It is they who inform Donna that a new planet has entered our Solar System.

In the waking world, unscrupulous agents are harvesting organs from coma victims. A new planet, which is bigger than Mars, is heading on a collision course towards Earth. Nothing in the conscious world can be done about that. But, increasingly, the border between the conscious world, and the world of dreams, is becoming more blurred. How can we tell what is real? How do we know we are really awake?

Previously, in Dark Forces:

GLADSTONE PARKS WAS in his office staring out of the window and talking to Geoff, who was at Armstrong Spaceport.

'Donna is in the bathroom' Geoff was saying. 'No facilities on the flight, well, except in a real emergency.'

Gladstone chuckled. 'Yes *some* things are rather difficult in zero gravity. I hope you have not had anything to eat or drink in the last hour; especially alcohol and fizzy drinks.'

'You know me Gladstone. I follow the rules slavishly.'

'Yeah, right! So how is Donna holding up?'

'Very well. She seems pretty much completely recovered from her unscheduled sleep.'

'I see. What about those strange dreams she had? I mean, has she managed to come to terms with all that?'

'Well she hasn't really revisited it. But if you are asking whether she believes she was dreaming it all up, the answer is no. She is not budging an inch. And I think you have to admit that it was rather spooky that she was right about Millie being on the moon, not to mention providing accurate facts about the new planet. Can you think of any possible way that she could have known those things? Let's face it Gladstone, this is all a bit *Twilight Zone*!'

Gladstone said 'Yes it is certainly far from business as usual. But there is no evidence that the new planet will come that close to us.'

Geoff said 'We must know its velocity by now surely? Then we could calculate precisely where it will intersect Earth's orbital path.'

'Yes, well that is the most bizarre thing of all. Our instruments are still not giving us readings.'

'Yes but what about telescopes. It must be child's play to track its progress by reference to the stars beyond and track its velocity.'

'They don't need us to tell them that Geoff! Apparently there is some kind of stellar phenomenon going on right now. It is not my field but Michigan says that there is a distortion effect, like a mirage, that makes it difficult to get an accurate fix on bodies at the edge of system and beyond. They likened it to the effect of the aurora-borealis from a visual point of view. But what it is, exactly, they don't know. The plain fact is, a lot of weird things are all happening at once. One of the Techies in Michigan even said that it what is going on out there beyond Pluto, is due to "curves in space" being caused by unnatural means! The rest of his colleagues say he is sometimes a bit crazy. He is though, the pre-eminent expert in his field. I'm dammed if I know.'

Then Geoff spotted Donna returning and said 'Ah, here she comes now.'

'Good, then wish her a good flight from me. Take good care of her and wish her all the best of luck seeing Millie. Someone will meet you on arrival whom I have had assigned for the duration of your visit. His name is David Coombes. He is a good man. Ok, safe flight, bye.'

Donna said 'Gladstone? How's he doing?'

'He seemed alright, but he is worried about your planet'

'*My* planet?'

'Well sure, you discovered it. It should be named "Donna." Why not? Venus was named after a feisty lady like you!'

'I don't think the goddess of love derived her reputation from being feisty!'

'Really? You need to re-discover your classics!'

'*Ping*! Ladies and Gentleman, Thank you for waiting. Apollo Spaceways kindly invites passengers travelling to New Shanghai on Lunar flight 411 to board at Gate 7. Bathroom facilities are available close to all gates. There are no bathroom facilities available on board this short flight. Also passengers are kindly reminded that eating and drinking is strictly prohibited while on board. This is a legal requirement.'

There were perhaps fifty or so passengers on the flight. As Geoff and Donna headed through the gate, Donna said, 'This is a monumental day in my life.'

Geoff said 'Yes, a person's first space flight, and first time to the moon. I think that qualifies as monumental.'

Donna said with a broad smile, 'True. But it is also my eighteenth birthday.'

'What! Donna you dark horse! You never mentioned a thing. Congratulations. You could have given me a hint. I haven't even got a card for you, let alone a present.'

'Are you kidding?' said Donna. 'You have got me a *space journey*. That is better than a card. And you have given me the chance to find Millie. There is no better present you could have given me. Not even close.' She took Geoff's hand momentarily, but had to let go, in order to board the craft, which was similar in design to a large passenger aircraft, superficially anyway.

There was no allocated seating. First come first served. They settled into a row for two, about halfway down the passenger cabin.

'I am excited', said Donna.'

'Actually so am I', said Geoff. 'This is my first time too.'

'Really!' said Donna. 'I should have thought this was a regular thing for you.'

'This is not a regular thing for *anybody*. I am glad there are still things you do not know having been brought into the "circle of trust" by those Architects!'

'It doesn't work that way' said Donna. 'You only hear what they want to tell you. In some ways, they leave you with more questions than answers. In a way, they help you realize how much you don't know. For example,...'

'*Ping*! Ladies and Gentlemen, welcome to Apollo Lunar Spaceways flight 411 to New Shanghai. I am Captain Hargreaves and it will be my pleasure to fly you to the moon today, along with my first officer,

Rupert Brooke. I am sorry there will no refreshments served on board, but the flight time is only thirty-three minutes, so I hope that will not inconvenience you. Please enjoy the flight.'

'What a lovely voice.' said Donna.

'Ping! Ladies and Gentleman, this is your Steward speaking. We will soon be underway. Smoking is strictly prohibited at any time during the flight. We would remind you, once again, that there are no bathroom facilities on board. You must wear your seatbelts at all times during the flight. Please do not leave your seats. No food or drink may be consumed at any time. There is CCTV in operation at all times. Please ensure that all items of hand-luggage are stowed in the overhead lockers. It is not permitted to have any items in the aisle, or stowed under your seat, or stowed on laps. These are legal requirements for your safety. Please adhere to all our safety requirements.'

'Blimey!' said Donna 'It's like, *Welcome onboard,* make yourself at home, *but stay there, don't put that there, and don't do this, or that, and not that, or else you will really be for it.*' They both laughed.

The laughing stopped abruptly as the Captain's voice rang out 'Kindly prepare for take-off'. The craft sprang forward dramatically. The taxi to this point had been so low-key as to go unremarked. But this sudden acceleration was very different. Donna felt her head pushed back against the head-rest. Within seconds the craft was flying at an angle of forty-five degrees, appreciably much more dramatic than passenger airlines.

'God' she said. 'I wasn't expecting this.' There was a little bit of turbulence, but Donna felt somewhat reassured by the force pushing her back into her seat because it felt resolute. Donna was thinking that something was missing; of course, the roar of the engines! There was none. The only sound was of the creaking of the fuselage. Donna looked at Geoff. He was looking out of his window but she noticed that he had a firm grip of the side-rest, as did she. She looked passed Geoff and, through the window, she saw thick grey clouds dispersing, to be replaced by bright sunshine and a clear blue sky. In moments however, the sky dimmed rapidly and became dark. Then she saw something that made her gasp. It was a star field of a million bright dots. Nothing had prepared her for how bright they were. And nothing had prepared her for what came next.

'Oh Lordy!' she exclaimed. We're falling! We're falling back down and we are going *upside down*. Oh my God. Whoa! I think I am going to throw up!' Geoff pushed a sick bag into her hand while grasping another for himself. Donna was convinced that they were falling backwards towards the Earth. She was too young to die! And what about Millie? What would happen to *her* now? Donna was gripping Geoff's hand, holding on for dear life. But a quick glance around the cabin revealed that nobody else seemed too concerned.

Geoff said 'It's alright. It is normal. It's just how weightlessness feels in space. We are not falling. It just feels like it. Take deep breaths. Nothing is going to happen. We're in space. That's all.'

'Yes' said Donna breathlessly. 'In space, *upside down!* That's all! No big deal!'

It took a while for pretty much everyone on board to adjust.

'Now I get it' Donna said. 'I mean, why they make so much fuss about not eating before or during the flight.' She retained her sick bag right in front of her.

'Here' said Geoff. 'Chew this. He handed her what looked like a chewy sweet.

'They give them out' he said, 'to be taken only if needed.' It was indeed needed, and it took effect quickly. Not only did her stomach cease to be a problem almost immediately, but she felt altogether calmer about everything.

'Gracious' she said. 'These things are really good. I feel great! Not a care in the world' Then she caught herself. 'Or *off* world either!'

Geoff grinned. He said 'Those *chewits* are not made available anywhere other than space. There is a maximum of one per person.'

'Are they addictive?' asked Donna.

'Oh yes, very. You can get as high as a lunar shuttle with a couple of those!' They sat in silence for a while. They were still adjusting to the strange feeling and staring out of the window, into a black field that now contained stars only. There were teeming millions of them. Twelve minutes into the voyage, Captain Hargreaves made a further announcement.

'Ladies and Gentleman, I just want to inform you that our indicator that relates to our retro-thrusters is not responding at this moment. There is nothing to be alarmed about. We are confident that the retro-thrusters are functioning normally. As I know you will be aware, the moon has only one-sixth of earth gravity. This makes things easier in many ways, but it does mean that the moon cannot hold on to an atmosphere. Unlike Earth, we cannot rely on air to slow us down to any degree, hence the need for retro-thrusters. This is likely to be an indicator light failure only. There has never been an occasion when the retro- thrusters have failed. Rest assured we shall have you down safely on time at 09.30 Lunar Mean Time. Please sit back and enjoy the rest of the flight.'

Donna said 'Well Captain Hargreaves does not sound unduly worried. Then again, I suppose he is trained to sound calm and reassuring.'

Geoff said 'I am sure that he *is* calm; particularly as he is AI.'

'He what?' exclaimed Donna. 'Are you telling me that we have no human crew on this flight?'

'Yes. Believe me, all transportation is safer without the possibility of human error looming over it. We are in safe hands with Captain Hargreaves. Well, not *hands*, but you know what I mean.'

'Gracious!' exclaimed Donna.

Geoff said 'Well why should *you* be worried. You have the Architects keeping an eye out for you!'

'I don't think they have any special interest in me. They have wider concerns. But I do wonder why they chose to share with *me* out of billions of others. I suppose that supports the theory that all of life is just a dream, in which case, of course, I would be the centre of the story. We all are; in our dreams.'

Geoff said 'Actually, that's an interesting point. Everybody is at the centre of their dream. But what actually happens in the dream-worlds, when two, or more people, are sharing a dream? The splicing of minds was not possible until Dreamcorp developed the technology for it. What was happening in the days before that, I mean with Seekers entering sleeper's dreams, was technically quite different. It was a less profound and immersive algorithmic intrusion. No, we at Dreamcorp, extended the dream-sharing facility by drawing upon, and stretching, Tarot's original design. Tarot, himself, was not there to sign-off on that extension. He had gone into a lasting coma by then. We actually made rather a lot of assumptions before we introduced that facility. Perhaps we screwed up.'

'How do you mean?'

'Well, what if splicing minds together, has had consequences in our brains? You were speaking of the unconscious mind as being special. It is certainly the most private part of our minds, I would say. Maybe having other people tramping around in it, has somehow affected nature's balance. How would we know except by things going wrong? And they have certainly been going wrong. I will call Emily about that after we land. Thank you for the steer.'

'You're welcome.'

'You know what Donna? I was not joking entirely when I mentioned that you could be valuable at Dreamcorp. Maybe the Architects singled you out for special treatment because you *are* special. I find it quite difficult to make friends. It sounds an awful thing to say but I find a lot of people very, well, ordinary. That is not to say that I do not have time for them, just, I don't know, I do not feel connected.

With you, I do. When we were together in the dream-suite, I could sense a huge amount of something in you, but I could not really label it at the time. There were a lot of distractions. But when you were talking at home, about the balance in everything, and the need for both good and evil in that equation, I realized what it was that you have in abundance; it's goodness. If I were an Architect, I would pick *you* to share with.'

'Wow, Geoff, saying things like that could make a girl fall in love with you! Be careful.'

Geoff looked at Donna. At that moment, she just looked vulnerable. Her big eyes reflected the soft blue lighting in the cabin and, as he looked at her, he wasn't sure whether the butterflies he felt in his stomach were due to the lack of gravity, or something closer to the heart.

'*Ping*! 'Ladies and Gentlemen, I am afraid I have some more rather bad news. Due to an incident in New Shanghai, we are being diverted to Leonov in the Lunar Northern Hemisphere, and arrangements will be made to complete your onward journeys from there.' There were moans of irritation. 'I must also inform you that the problems with our retro-thrusters may be worse than we initially thought. It is possible that we may not have the evenly disposed retro- effect required for a smooth landing. Purely as a precaution, we have declared an emergency. On approach to landing I will ask you to lower your heads as far as possible in a brace position. I stress this is a precaution. Confidence remains high that we will be able to make a controlled landing. Please stand by for further instructions.'

Geoff muttered 'Instructions rather than requests. I don't like the sound of that!' Then he looked at Donna's worried expression. 'But I am sure it will be ok' he added. 'As he said, retro-thrusters have never failed before.'

Donna said 'Let us hope the phrase *first time for everything* does not apply here.' She was grateful for the effects of the chewy sweet that

Geoff had given her. She doubted that she would have been able to remain quite so calm without it. She said 'Just for the record Geoff, there's a lot of goodness in you too. I was thinking that we had all the time in the world, but maybe the story is going to play out differently. I'm scared, Geoff.' She took his hand.

Then something happened. The feeling in the pit of their stomachs changed and they could feel that the vessel was acquiring a different angle. For the first time since leaving Earth's orbit, there was a faint hint of which direction was down.

'*Ping*! Ladies and Gentlemen, we are on our final approach. Please ensure that your seat belts are secured tightly and be ready to take the brace position when I say so.'

Their eyes were drawn to the windows, hungrily seeking out a runway. They were looking for those familiar lines of runway lights, but there was nothing visible now, not even the stars. There was, however, a feeling of deceleration, and a stronger sense of a weak, but tangible, gravity.

There was no '*ping*'. Without warning the Captain said 'This is going to be very bumpy. Remember to take deep breaths. Lower your heads between your knees now. **Brace Brace Brace**.'

Chapter 1

Leonov City. The Moon

'BRACE BRACE BRACE'

Donna and Geoff let go hands and lowered their heads. They were unable to see the emergency vehicles lining each side of the runway. After years of chopping and changing, landings on the moon followed the traditional airline method of landing on runways, despite the fact that there was no air to support the wings that were essential for take-offs and landings back on Earth. Rocket launches had been abandoned, except for exploration of Mars and beyond. But whichever landing method was used, retro-thrusters were an absolute requirement.

Nobody at all was speaking. Most were praying. There is a moment when a person feels in peril for their life when their thoughts invariably turn from material concerns, and reach out for the comfort of something beyond our mortal end. The survival instinct works in an extra-ordinary way. When there is something that one can do to survive, it becomes imperative to do it. It typically supersedes everything else except in some cases, and quite remarkably, the desire to save a loved one first. But in cases where survival is definitely outside of one's control, as in this case, the human mind still cannot believe that it is all over. Instead the mind thinks of all sorts of other scenarios, the most common being survival and being taken to hospital. So long as there is life, there is hope. And Donna and Geoff were doing nothing but hoping when they felt the nose of the craft angling upwards for landing, so that the back wheels would touch first. But in this case, "touch" was the wrong word. The wheels crashed onto the runway, and they could feel the back of the craft springing upwards behind them. Now they were nose forward to the runway, and only metres from it, but moving at a speed more than ten times normal for that distance from the ground. The silence was broken, as pretty much every passenger let out shouts and screams. Donna was holding her brace position so tightly that just about everything hurt. She was so tense, waiting for the nose to hit the ground. But instead, the craft started to move back into a horizontal position and, shortly after that, the nose went up once more and they realized that they were climbing again. They continued to climb on a straight course and then started to bank to the left. In reduced gravity, spacecraft are able to bank much more sharply, and so it was here. The craft seemed to be leaning almost completely on its side. Now people came out of the brace positions. Geoff and Donna could see the lights on the lunar surface, through the window. It felt weird and frightening looking out of a side window and seeing the lit spaceport directly below them.

Gradually, the craft straightened up, and the Captain spoke again. 'Ladies and Gentlemen, as you will have noticed, it was necessary to abort that landing. Apollo Spaceways apologizes sincerely for any discomfort. We are going to make a second landing attempt in a few minutes. Due to fuel concerns, we will only be able to make one further landing attempt. The additional time has given emergency facilities more time to prepare. Due to lessons learned from our first attempt, we are going to land a little in advance of the runway on the partially prepared strip. This will be bumpy, but it is necessary as a means to help reduce velocity and not to overshoot the spaceport boundary. Once again, sincere apologies for this, and please listen for my " Brace" command. Good luck to us all.'

There was a sense of déjà vu as they descended. The hefty jolt in the first aborted landing attempt had reduced just about everybody's level of confidence, which had not been that high. Now there was more of an air of inevitability. Donna said to Geoff. 'If I don't make it, please just tell my Mom that I love her!' And she thought: Does everybody want to say *I love you* to someone at the end?

Geoff said 'We are going to make it Donna, I promise you.'

The Captain's voice cut in, 'OK, again. Brace. Brace. Brace'.

CRASH!!

The back wheels smashed down, and there was a very loud mechanical screeching sound. The whole craft shook violently as the terrain punished the wheels. At least they would not catch fire, with no air to feed it. This time, the nose did not raise up, but the shuddering and bouncing was terrifying, and that was compounded by a feeling that they were moving at an awkward angle. In the next moment, they felt the front wheels set down, but less dramatically than the back ones. The fuselage was shaking violently. People were screaming. Every overhead locker had burst open and there was stuff everywhere. Some were hit by it, but nobody could see what was going on, because they were still very much in brace positions. With no retro-thrusters functioning, the brakes were hardly making any difference. Everybody was preparing for the worst. Donna's mind turned to the Architects. She was thinking: What was the point of talking to me if I am going to die! What's the point of anything? Then Donna felt a most unusual sensation. It was like she was being enveloped in warm breath, and she felt both dizzy and relaxed.

Suddenly it felt like they had hit something. Involuntarily, Donna and Geoff sat up. In fact, there had been no impact. The retro-thrusters had fired simultaneously on maximum power. The deceleration effect was so strong that the seatbelts really dug in and hurt. But miraculously, they slowed to a complete stop. For a moment there was absolute silence on board Apollo 411. Then people started to groan and move. Everybody was checking to see whether they had been injured and to what extent.

Geoff said 'Silly question, but are you alright?'

'I think so. I feel very shaky, and I hurt in a lot of places, especially around my middle.'

'Alright, well the moon is essentially the biggest hospital in the known universe, and they will definitely be giving us all the full works.'

In just a matter of moments, AI medics had boarded the craft and were effortlessly lifting some injured passengers into waiting ambulances.

Geoff had been quite right. The moon had far more than its fair share of hospitals. The reduced gravity created conditions that were suited to so many kinds of treatment, including most kinds of serious surgical procedures. Less gravity meant less strain on the heart and, in fact, less strain on every part of our anatomy. Nearly forty percent of visitors to the moon came for medical reasons. The large customer base of people recuperating, coupled with lunar conditions, made for a thriving business in medical facilities including convalescent homes and rejuvenating health spas. The lower gravity and richly oxygenated facilities, where all manner of harmful bacteria were screened out, made for first rate opportunities for salt baths and bathing, in what had become known as 'moon-dust'. Healing properties had been found in the soil on the moon. The same products were hugely expensive on earth. Treatments with moon-dust were not only fashionable but proven to have a range of dermatological benefits as well as helping heal deep muscle fissures and bone disorders. The health market attracted a range of ancillary markets, particularly sports and leisure. Again here, reduced gravity meant that people wishing to indulge in a gradual build up in exercise, meant that they could do so much more safely. This was particularly the case for those with heart conditions.

Now it was Donna and Geoff's turn to be assisted out of the craft through the main door, and through a giant connecting tube, into a large lunar vehicle. Although it served as an ambulance, it was very much bigger than its Earth counterparts. It was more of a mobile paramedic unit, where synthetics and syncopated machinery could treat multiple patients at once.

Donna and Geoff were surprised and delighted when the medics gave them both a clean bill of health. In fact, it turned out that they were the only passengers that were not required to stay in hospital overnight. The AI doctor said that he had rarely seen such robust conditions following any kind of trauma.

'You are very lucky young people', said the doctor. 'Somebody must be watching over you. Enjoy the rest of your lives, and don't waste it.'

'Did you *see* that?' said Donna' He winked! Do synthetics do that?'

'Evidently, they do' said Geoff. And our doctor was latest gen. He is a 238 model. They only came out last year. Well, let's see if we can find our reception committee and, well, get on with the rest of our lives!'

The first thing they needed to learn, was how to moon-walk. It was indeed completely different. Weighing so little felt really strange.

Donna said 'I must weigh now, what I did when I was an infant. But I don't ever remember feeling this light. I feel insecure – or should I say – *unsecured* as though I might just blow away. Why didn't it feel this way the last time I weighed so little?'

Geoff replied 'It is about the mass to gravity relationship. When you were little and weighed less on Earth, your mass was much less. The change in gravity has affected our usual mass to weight ratio. We are not used to it. Lunar dwellers do adjust. When they visit Earth, they complain that it seems like carrying a wardrobe around all the time! So for us, it feels a bit similar to walking around in a swimming pool up to our chests.'

'A bit similar, but far from the same', said Donna.' As they reached the main terminal building via the underground moving walkway, David Coombes met them. Possibly being influenced by the name, Geoff was expecting a younger version of Gladstone Parks, in a bright suit and tie. In fact, David was from Pakistan and was wearing a striking white garment, with intricate stitch work, of a type similar to that worn at prayer by Muslims. David spoke with a really odd blend of a Pakistani accent, and that of an old-fashioned English Colonial voice. It was as if the two vocal styles were battling for supremacy.

'Oh, thank goodness that you are alright! You look in wonderful shape, considering. How are you feeling? My God, what a thing to happen! And on your very first trip to the moon! Do you know that *nobody* was killed? The first and, pray God, only crash on the moon, and nobody was killed; not even seriously hurt. It is a miracle. God be praised!'

Geoff said 'Yes indeed. We are doing alright, thank you. Well, better than alright, and very grateful to be here!'

'Yes, yes, thank God. And you are the lovely Donna. Your reputation precedes you.'

'My reputation?' said Donna 'Do I have one of those?'

'Do you have a reputation? Are you joking? You are smoking hot news!

Do you not know that the President of the United States called you by name in his National address? OK, no, maybe not. It was just after you took off on your journey here.'

Donna said 'I don't understand.'

David said 'You *discovered* the new planet Donna. Everybody in the word is going to know your name by this time tomorrow. You not only discovered a planet that is heading straight for us, but the story is out that you did it in your sleep!'

Geoff said 'Yes, that is going to complicate things.'

David said 'Oh yes. At this moment there is nobody who is more famous than you are. You are celebrity, and you have no idea how much pressure there is on me to take care of you! There are pictures of you, Donna, on screens from here to the Martian colonies. The President of China, Ms Lee, wants to meet you! Come, let us get you to your hotel. Don't worry about your bags, they will be sent on, and there is no need to pass security; you have the same as temporary diplomatic status. Now, I must warn you, we have done our best, but reporters may have already found out where you are. If they reach you just say, "No comment." If you answer, you will be surrounded. They are synthetics mostly, so don't worry about disappointing them. They have a job to do, so perhaps you will agree to talk to them later, but on your own terms, and after we have briefed you on a few things. I began my days as a journalist, so I understand their point of view also. Life is hard and sometimes dangerous for them, but it is also very difficult for people who become overnight celebrities. No time to adjust. Yes, very difficult!'

Donna said 'I can hardly believe what you are saying. How can things have moved that quickly? I understand about the planet, of course, but they will soon forget about me.'

David said 'No, no. That will not be the case.'

Geoff said 'No, I agree Donna. What you are, and what you represent is very big news. Your life is now in the public domain.'

'Oh come on!'

David said 'Donna, there are images of you everywhere. You are a very striking young lady as it is, and already momentum is building. Some people are calling you supernatural! My God, there are already people who think that you can save us from a collision with the new planet!'

'I can't believe it' said Donna 'One minute I am having a dream. The next, I am on a spaceship to the moon. Then the spaceship crashes and then I find that my face is everywhere!' Maybe I am still in that dream. Pinch me hard Geoff.'

'I assure you that you are not dreaming' said David. But you are right. Since people became aware of you; you, and all your fellows have survived the *only* crash landing on the moon. You are *even more* famous. We are going to have to change plans and schedule. You certainly cannot go to New Shanghai at this time. No, certainly not.'

Donna said 'What do you mean? We are here to find Millie as soon as possible.'

David said 'Well, yes, but "as soon as possible" may not be for a few days at least.'

Geoff said 'Really! Are things that dramatic?'

David said 'The panic on the Earth is not half what it is here. Lunar dwellers are inclined to feel more paranoid at the best of times, being isolated from mother Earth. But with talk of tidal waves that may sweep the moon out of orbit and out into space – or towards the sun - well, things are getting very tense very quickly. There is no transportation to New Shanghai. That is out of the question. There are riots going on there! No, I'm sorry. We are in lockdown mode for the time being.'

Donna said 'My sole purpose here is to find Millie and ensure her safety.'

David said 'That is completely understood. But *your* safety is my first concern. Unless you can make your own way south without breathing air, you cannot get there for now. Nobody can. Please be patient. Millie is alright. She is at Verne, and the treatment there is first class.'

Donna said 'It is the treatment that I am worried about!'

They were now travelling along a moving walk-way while they were talking. David said 'We're nearly there. Let me fill you in about things here, although you probably know – but just in case. You were diverted from New Shanghai in the Southern Hemisphere which is home to the bulk of the Lunar population. This city, Leonov, is much smaller and more exclusive. It caters mostly to a grouping of gambling consortia, hospitals, spas, and health resorts. Some people call it the Monte Carlo of the moon. The most famous tourist destination on the moon is right next door to your hotel; the Icarus crater. But you will not want to go there today, I am sure. Although by tomorrow, you will probably be too well known to go. Ah, here we are. Let's get you checked in and give you some time to relax and freshen up. You look well, but you have had a hell of an ordeal.'

As they passed into the lobby there was commotion. There was a palpable tension and the screens were full of reporters with a depiction of a planet on the screen behind them. There was no volume, but a tapering strap line at the bottom of the screen read: *Alarm and civil unrest spreading in major cities across the globe as tensions and speculation rise.*

David ushered them straight into an elevator. 'We have arranged check-in for you already. Don't worry, everything is taken care of.' David led them into a room that looked part office and part mini-lounge. There were drinks and snacks laid out, and there was an en-suite. David said 'It is still morning and your rooms are not quite ready yet, sorry; just a short while. Will you excuse me a minute, I need to call in.' He left.

Donna said 'He seems a nice man.'

Geoff replied 'Since Gladstone gave him the thumbs up, I think he must be,' and he mimicked his voice, 'a top draw chap!' Donna smiled.

Geoff continued 'Obviously I have not met him previously, but I do know something of him. As a Pakistani man he took an Indian wife and she was a civilian casualty of the India-Pakistan border skirmishes.'

Donna said 'On no! She died?'

'Yes.'

'Does he have children?'

Yes, a boy and a girl, both still young.'

'Oh, for heaven's sake!'

David returned and handed them their electric key cards. He said, 'I know it's morning our time, but perhaps you should get some rest given the time difference with New York time.'

Geoff did not even look at Donna 'Actually we are not tired at all, quite the reverse. In a sense, we have been given a new lease of life. But we could do with some time to freshen up.'

David said 'In any event, I shall withdraw and leave you in peace for the rest of the day. This hotel is huge with every facility. If you like you could relax in the spa or try the pool. Swimming in one-sixth gravity is an experience not to miss. You have my number. Perhaps we could meet for breakfast tomorrow morning? OK. See you later. Call me for anything.'

After he departed Donna said 'So shall we go and settle in, and then meet maybe here afterwards?'

'Yes, good. How long do you need?'

'Not long. A half hour?'

'Fine'

Donna examined the key-card and said 'How about that! Our rooms are on different floors. Do you think the Fates are trying to tell us something?'

'Perhaps the Architects!' said Geoff.

WHEN THEY RECONVENED, they were at a bit of a loss as to what to do. They nibbled on a few assorted snacks until Donna said, 'Well since we cannot press on for the time being, what are we going to do?'

Geoff said 'We could try the pool. That would probably be relaxing.'

Donna said 'Do you want to relax, I don't. I'm hyper. After what we experienced today, and with not being able to any closer to Millie, whatever I am feeling, it is not relaxed. We need a big distraction to keep us occupied.'

Geoff said 'You're not thinking..... ...?'

'Why not? It's right next door, the man said. And he said tomorrow would be more difficult. They say the best way to recover after a flying accident is to fly again. So, let's fly!'

'Seriously?'

'Yep! We've already crashed today. Now I want to fly! I don't want to be brooding about Millie until I can *actually* do something.'

'Alright, if you're absolutely sure, let's go.'

Chapter 2.

Icarus Crater, The Moon

THE ICARUS CRATER WAS exactly that. It was a *crater* five miles in diameter covered by an enormous dome. On entering the voluminous space, they encountered a huge statue of Arthur C Clarke. 'It was his idea about doming craters', said Geoff.

Donna said 'I know, I read his books. He predicted how the moon might be developed and he was right on all counts, including the hospitals. I love Arthur C.'

The dome was lovely and warm. The pinnacle at the top of the ceiling was nearly three miles above their heads. Powerful warm air thermals were being blasted upwards from machines below grills on the floor of the crater. As they looked up, they could see maybe a hundred people flying like birds, with wings. It looked like a lot of skill was required.

A man approached them from behind. 'Would you like to try it?' he asked.

'Perhaps not', said Geoff. 'We have only just arrived and didn't know what to expect. It obviously takes practice and skill that we do not have.'

'You are right about that.' said the man who was obviously a synthetic. 'It is like skiing and ocean surfing, but whereas those sports are only for the experienced, this can be enjoyed by pretty much anyone. If they are reasonably healthy.' he added. 'And you both look both well and fit'.

Donna took on a puzzled expression. The guide continued 'We have trained *gondoliers* who can take one passenger each, and fly with them. It's perfectly safe. Distancing rules apply with wide margins for error and it is impossible to crash.' Geoff looked at Donna.

'No' Geoff said, 'I still think it is pretty dangerous.' Better to give it a miss, and just watch, I think.

'It's free of charge' said the man. 'The first one is always free because everyone wants to do it again. This is the only place you can do this. The low gravity, high roof-dome, and warm thermals combination, means that the wingspan lets you fly like a bird; something that mankind has always yearned do. Every generation until now has missed out. You may never get the chance again! You are never truly free until you have conquered fear.' This last sentence acted as a trigger.

'Let's do it', said Donna. 'Come on. Let's just do it.'

DONNA AND GEOFF EMERGED from the elevator close to the top of the crater, behind a small group of people, who were being encouraged into lines that resembled queues at airports, before passing through security. Donna could see that each person was being harnessed to a *gondolier*. Up close, they were a bit intimidating. They were perhaps three metres tall, and in place of arms, they had wings of nearly four metres in length. Otherwise shaped like humanoids, they had an androgynous appearance, and their heads were graced by something fashioned like a face but with mere impressions for a nose and mouth. Small eyes resembled vacant sockets.

'Are you sure about this?' asked Geoff. 'It's not too late to turn around.' Donna just nodded and faced front.

When it happened, it happened quickly. Donna was harnessed to a *gondolier* and found herself standing on what resembled a giant springboard. She glanced behind her, and was reassured to see Geoff similarly harnessed to a *gondolier* who towered over him. She barely had time to turn her head to face front again, before her synthetic transport sprang forward and upwards. They were climbing in a blanket of warm air. Whereas she had anticipated some discomfort wearing a harness, there was none at all. Here she weighed little more than a cat. They were moving upwards, in a spiral around the wall of the crater. Donna could see that the whole of the centre section was filled with independent fliers – no *gondoliers* necessary. Men and women with wings attached to their arms were moving expertly. Some were doing aerobatics. She recalled something she had heard some time ago on the news. From next year this was to be an Olympic Sport. The Olympic Committee had admitted the first new sport in over ten years. Some of those people out there might soon be making history. Or perhaps, with the uncertainty surrounding the new planet in mind, maybe not!

Now they had reached their highest point. They were still some distance from the ceiling and, if anything, the air felt denser and reassuring. Of course it would. Heat rises. Now began a gentle descent, still in a spiral, and Donna could see Geoff flying just on the inside of her, close enough to see his smile. He was watching her like a hawk and he looked like one! Now there was a dramatic change. The walls of the dome that had looked grey and dull suddenly burst into colour. A high-resolution 3D effect gave the impression of flying over an alien jungle that stretched for miles in every direction, with huge white and blue mountains, and lakes of bright orange. The illusion was so comprehensive that there was nothing to suggest that they were actually inside a lunar crater at all. It was like flying on another planet in another eco-system altogether. Donna did not doubt the man's words earlier. Anybody would want to do this again and again. This was life affirming. It was glorious. It made her spirit soar, as she herself soared. The only downside was that it had to end. Now came a change. Instead of continuing to descend, they started to ascend again. Donna could feel the pumping of the wings and looked over to see Geoff, still shadowing her, as they actually accelerated upwards, bolstered by the reassuring warm thermals. Then there were a few moments when they were flying level, side by side. Donna gasped as she saw Geoff's *gondolier* dive, straight down, like a bird of prey. But within seconds, she too was plummeting down, and right on Geoff's tail like a fighter in a dog-fight. Having experience zero gravity in space, this dive, pushing into a pillow of warm air, felt absolutely lovely. Donna was thinking at that very moment of how she would describe this sensation to her mother, knowing that words would never be adequate to convey it properly. It *had* to be experienced. She could not recall ever having felt more alive, than that moment.

The landing was as soft as tissue paper.

'I'm really glad we did that.' said Donna. 'I feel really invigorated; like I could climb a mountain.'

Geoff said 'That is the combination of adrenalin and the fact that this dome has about fifteen percent more oxygen than Earth. You are getting an oxygen fix.' Donna's cheeks were certainly flushed.

As they exited the dome area, Donna realized that they were holding hands. She really hadn't noticed. She looked at Geoff. They had dreamt together. They had flown together. They had nearly been killed together, and now they were alive together, positively fizzing with energy. But now they needed to find Millie. It didn't mean anything, if they failed at that. Geoff looked at her as though he could read her thoughts. But since they were not in a dream-world at that moment, he could not.

When they got back to the hotel, things looked rather different. Four police guarded the entrance. These were large androids that would have weighed as much as five men on Earth. It was well known that police, and all emergency services on the moon, were run by one private company *Sentinel Security, Chiswick*. The moon was the only populated land area that was not under any sovereign jurisdiction. It was a free-trade zone that had been established by huge multi-nationals, and no Government had been able to establish jurisdiction. Even attempts to step in by the UN, had been robustly rebuffed.

As Geoff and Donna entered the hotel, they could see from the giant wall-screens, that the protests on the moon had escalated. The tag-line along the bottom read that hysteria was growing and that this kind of escalation on the moon had never been envisaged. There was simply not enough policing resource available. A receptionist caught Donna's attention and pointed to the lobby bar. Apparently, there was a package waiting there for her.

When she entered the bar with Geoff at her side, a group of staff sang "Happy Birthday" to a contrapuntal standard that only synthetics could attain. They presented her a small cake, with eighteen red candles, and a heart in the middle. She looked at Geoff. 'How did you manage this? I have had my eye on you the whole time.' Geoff replied, 'Never underestimate a Dreamcorp man,' and handed her a glass of champagne. 'Happy eighteenth!'

Donna said, 'I suppose you are going to tell me that this comes from the champagne region under a crater here on the moon?'

Geoff laughed 'Certainly not. There are things that the moon is most definitely not suitable for. This is from the Champagne region of France; copied, but never bettered. Oh, and,' He produced a box of Belgian chocolates from behind his back. Donna put one arm around him, drew him in, and kissed the side of his neck. They sat by the expansive window looking out over the lunar landscape that was flood-lit in interleaving blue and white patterns so that it looked much like a shimmering lake. They chinked glasses. 'Can I ask you something Geoff?'

'Of course, go ahead.'

Donna did not look into his eyes. 'Well, the thing is, sometimes, I feel that you are maintaining a sort of, well, professional distance from me. Is that true?'

Geoff shifted a bit uncomfortably in his chair. 'Look Donna,' he said, 'Don't get me wrong. I like you - very much. But the thing is, I am technically at work right now, and besides that....'

'Yes?'

'Well, you have such a lot on your plate at the moment, right? I mean, leaving aside your recent coma, and all this stuff going on out there about this new planet, or whatever it is; you are still really worried about Millie and we have a job ahead of us. I just don't think this would be a good time to make things any more complicated. Quite frankly, and don't forget that I have been in your mind, I don't think you want that either. Not now. Maybe soon. I *hope* soon. But not now.'

Now Donna looked directly into his eyes. 'You're right of course. I am too wound up about Millie to be clear in my mind about anything right now.' She slid her hand gently into his. 'I'm glad we talked about this. I wouldn't want you to misunderstand my feelings for you either. I'm glad you are so smart Geoff. It makes life easier.' She undid the blue ribbon on her chocolates, and slowly lifted one into Geoff's mouth. Then she swiftly popped another into her mouth, and and her face took on an expression of ecstasy. She said 'You know what Geoff, after mankind has travelled faster than light and explored the Universe, it just might be that the nicest things were always right here on Earth. Perhaps we should be appreciating it more and taking better care of what we have!'

Geoff just looked at her, marvelling at how quickly that Donna was blossoming.

After a while, just gazing at the view of the Lunar surface while sipping Champagne and munching chocolate, Donna said 'Goodness, I am suddenly very tired now. I think the time difference has caught up with me —or perhaps the Champagne. It has been a lovely birthday - Lunar crashes aside - and thank you for making it so special, Geoff. Will you walk me to my door?' Then she glanced at her cake sitting on a nearby table. She had forgotten to blow out the candles, but they had burned down. The flames had reached higher in low gravity and burned faster in more oxygen. The sentiment, however, was the same in any conditions.

Chapter 3

Dream-world. Dystopia

CLOISTERED IN THE KEEP, Clovis was wandering between groups of Jeebers, and what he was saying was inaudible. But Martin and Rio knew exactly what he was saying. They could sense the emotions he was expressing. He was using calming words, but he was not deceiving them. The security provided by the door was that of a vault, with a long sheer drop acting as a moat. There was practically no chance that any deranged Jeebers would be able to surmount that. But there was another concern. As sound as the fortifications were, they were not proof against the aliens themselves. Those shapeless forms were not affected by gravity, and seemed to be able to pass through walls. The biggest danger was that the aliens would reach across any barriers and insinuate themselves into the minds of the otherwise peacefully assembled Jeebers. This was the more disquieting because the person one trusted the most, could be, in the next instant, in a killing frenzy. The effect of this alien technique was that it was difficult to really trust anyone.

Rio watched Clovis, and wondered about how he had become a leader among these people. Martin answered as if she had raised a question aloud 'It was the strength of his mind. Not just his resolve and organizational skills or even his charisma, which is extraordinary, but just the sheer strength of his mind. You can feel it can't you?'

Rio said with a thoughtful expression 'Yes. You and Clovis both have that sort of inner strength. It's very reassuring. I wonder if Clovis is his real name. It sounds more like a nickname.'

K said. 'It is the name he goes under here. But you might remember the name from what some call the "dark ages". In the time the Roman Empire was fragmenting, a figure called Clovis united the various factions of the Francs against the marauding hordes of Goths, Visigoths and other assailants. The French still regard him as the man who founded France, out of the vestiges of Trans-Alpine Gaul and a part of Germania, as was.'

Rio was intrigued by K's knowledge. She tested the waters a little further.

'What year was this?'

K replied 'He was *de facto* King of the Franks from 481 to 511AD.

'

Corvette joined in. She said 'What is most interesting about Clovis is that he devised a portal between what we understand as life, and death. The portal was destroyed when marauders attempted to use it as a weapon. History records that Clovis died in 511 but he was seen by many, alive, in 513. For someone of such renown at the time, it is extraordinary to have such a lack of clarity about the date of death, and yet there were so many witnesses to his reappearance or resurrection. Years later, there was also confusion about whether his remains had been correctly identified. By the time that his vaunted remains were "relocated" to Saint Denis Basilica in 1768, he was being referred to as one of the "acolytes". The cult members that revered the acolytes were hunted and killed for heresy, and nearly all records of them expunged. The cult re-emerged centuries later.'

Rio said 'I see. So, who were these so called acolytes?'

Corvette replied 'They were a group of people who turned up at different times in human history, and were most notable for making remarkable contributions well before their time. Examples include the Greek philosopher Democritus from the fifth century BC. He postulated that matter was made up of atoms. He described the nature and motion of atoms as the building blocks of matter as we understand them today. He even gave them their name "Atoma", being the indivisible foundation of matter. As a matter of fact, he was more accurate than even most scientists realize. When he spoke of *atoma* he was not meaning atoms as such, but rather he was referring to the atomic particles that make up the atom. It was not until the end of the twentieth century that scientists caught up with him. He was a quantum physicist when most people still dwelt in caves and huts. He also accurately described *the void* at a time when conventional thinking was that the sky was the home of the gods. He was considered mad at the time, but proven correct two and a half thousand years later.'

Rio said 'This is a brilliant distraction. I want to keep my mind occupied. Please go on.'

Corvette continued 'Perhaps the most famous of the acolytes was Leonardo da Vinci, who died in 1519. His innovations encompassed major advances in engineering, astronomy, anatomy, botany, cartography, palaeontology, aerodynamics, hydrodynamics, optics, geology and mathematics. His concepts embraced aircraft, including helicopters and fighter planes; calculators, and solar power, among others. For all that, he was most renowned as a painter. The Mona Lisa is the most famous piece of art in history. It is enigmatic and in recent times it has been called "a depiction of consciousness." It eludes all analysis as to why it should have such universal appeal. Some of the materials that would have been required to manufacture da Vinci's designs were not discovered or invented during his lifetime. The latter-day acolyte cults maintained that the likes of Democritus, Da Vinci, and Abel Levinson, the latter having divined and defined the nature of reality in the Nineteenth century, were a select group of humans whose minds were said to have been touched by a higher intelligence than mankind. Levinson disappeared without trace and was putatively deleted from recorded history. Knowledge of his existence comes from a single source: Tarot, the architect of dreams.'

'I have heard of Tarot.' said Martin. I thought that he was a made up story.'

K said 'By no means. Tarot is considered by some to be the latest of the acolytes. He advanced the digital horizon massively in one giant leap. His mind was such that he mastered every branch of science and did what nobody else was able to: develop a comprehensive overview of the mechanics of creation. His innovations included transplanting the human mind into a synthetic body; transferring consciousness into micro-processors so small that they could be stored in atomic particles; divining the true nature of consciousness; understanding the relationship between thought, and energy and matter; and divining the true nature of reality'.

'Golly!' said Martin. He was clearly an extra-ordinary guy. But sadly he's dead now right?'

Corvette said 'No. But his whereabouts is withheld.'

'Withheld?' said Rio. 'That's a strange term especially for a person of such renown. Withheld by whom?'

'That information is classified' Corvette said.

Rio said 'The plot thickens. K and Corvette, I must say that your knowledge of all this stuff is truly impressive.'

Martin looked at Rio, sighed, and said 'Nobody could claim that I surround myself with bimbos!'

Rio decided to check something out. She asked 'K, do you know what 562.3 divided by 66 comes to?'

'Yes. 8.51'

'Is that right?' she asked Martin.

'Absolutely no idea' he answered.

'Yes' said Corvette. 'It is correct to two decimal places. 8.5196969697 to ten places.'

'As I thought.' said Rio to Martin. 'Remind me not to play them at chess Martin!'

Without warning, there was a very deep boom that vibrated all around. Rio looked across at Martin. His relaxed demeanour had been replaced by the look of a father trying to protect his family from an imminent threat. But nothing further happened. All remained quiet for a long while and everybody settled down again. With her breathing returned to normal, Rio asked, 'So where were you born, Martin?'

He replied 'I am not sure. Somewhere in East Africa, I think.'

'Go on. I want to learn about you.'

'It is not a nice story. It's quite difficult actually.'

Rio said, 'Well I will not press you, but I am actually interested.'

'Alright, well, my parents were both killed in violence in front of me. Trucks pulled into our village one morning and some bandit militia killed almost everyone. I was struck on the head and woke up later in a military hospital. I had not been badly wounded but apparently I had been unconscious for quite a while. Shortly after that, the hospital was attacked by mortar fire. Nearly everybody was killed. Again, I do not remember much after that, except I was moved through makeshift field hospitals and refugee camps. Finally I was resettled in Seattle. I was adopted but I don't remember too much about my new parents or the house, except fragments. They were kind though. I remember I could see a mountain from my widow. I have blanks in my memory. I have been told that this is due to the trauma I witnessed as a child.' Rio could see the distress in Martin's expression. She could also feel it, palpably – like it was her own.

'I would much rather hear about you.' he said.

Rio said 'Well, I did not experience anything as traumatic as you. Not until' she faltered 'not until this, here. But I am the same as you when it comes to memories. It does not flow like a continuous story. All I remember from my childhood was my sister, and living in Greenwich Village in New York. I remember the bagels and the roasted chestnuts that they used to sell on the corner of Bleaker. I was stalked by some creep on the subway once. He followed me from carriage to carriage.

When he reached me, I thought he was going to pull out a knife. I was really scared. He leaned right in, but then he just, sort of, clutched his chest and died right in front of me. He just keeled over, right at my feet. I never touched him. I had to give the cops a statement. They searched him and actually did find a knife; a big one. It turned out that he had stabbed and killed two women before, but apparently the evidence against him was bungled somehow and he got off. Anyway, there were three eye-witnesses to his assault on me, and they confirmed that he had just died of his exertions I suppose. Maybe he had a weak heart! The strange thing is when I got home Vanessa was there, absolutely frantic with worry. Nobody had contacted her and there was no way she could have known anything, but she was in a terrible state. She absolutely knew that something had happened although she did not know what. I started reading about telepathy between twins after that. So did Vanessa. I really miss her. She is like the other side of me. She is more serious than I am; not so much of a joker, although she loves a good laugh.

As a matter of fact, nobody I meet these days seems to have coherent memories. Well, except K and Corvette of course! I have a theory that we all live in a series of realities, that link up in different ways, at different times. I must admit though, that something is troubling me about Vanessa right now. You see, even if I have no idea where she is, I always know that she is *somewhere*. I do not feel it exactly, I just know. But very recently, it has been like having an empty space where she used to be. I can't explain it. But I feel cold inside when I think about her. I think I might have to face up to the fact, at some point, that she might have died.

'She is not dead.' said Clovis who had come up on them without being noticed from along the side.

'How do you know?' asked Rio.

'I m not sure that I can explain.' he replied. 'When I met you I sensed her. I sense her now. In some ways it is like you are two sides of the same coin.'

'That's exactly right', said Martin. 'I was aware of Vanessa the moment I felt Rio's mind open.'

Martin said to Clovis 'They are like Siamese twins. Not joined in the body, of course, but joined in the mind. One is always with the other in that sense. If you know one, you sort of know them both.'

'I am *here, you know'* said Rio. 'Where I come from it is considered rude to talk about someone who is present!'

'Yes, of course' said Martin, looking at Clovis. 'Sorry, I got a bit carried away.'

Clovis said 'Yes sorry. But we have turned a corner today. We are three people who are capable, not only of holding our ground against the enemy minds, but combining our energies against them. We met by sheer chance and yet our minds are capable of meshing in a manner I would not have thought possible.'

Rio said 'I am not convinced about the meeting by sheer chance bit. But it is undeniable that we are stronger when we combine in the way that we did. Collectively, we are much stronger. In a sense, this is a numbers game. We need more minds like ours to stand any chance against them.'

Everybody remained quiet for a few moments and then Clovis said 'Having your sister with us would make a real difference.'

'Yes, it would probably help.' said Rio.

Clovis looked across at Martin and said, 'I don't think she knows!'

Rio ran a hand through her hair 'I don't know what?'

Martin made eye contact with Clovis 'What Clovis is saying is that when we three are together we are stronger in combination, but when you and Vanessa combine...'

'Yes?'

'Well, we can sense it. It's obvious. If you two were to combine as we just did then, I don't know, between you there would be a lot more energy created.'

Rio said 'Well that makes sense. With Vanessa and I together, we could double our, whatever it is that we have. I am not sure there is a word for it.'

Martin said 'No Rio - not double. I think we are talking about millions of times more energy!'

'What? That's insane. How could you know something like that or even think it?'

Clovis said 'You yourself saw what just happened in that elevator, and you were part of it. Would you have believed any of it was possible just one week ago? Would you have believed that your mind could be a powerful weapon? You accept that, but you doubt how far it could extend if you were to be joined with your sister. You are really only questioning the extent or degree of a phenomenon that by reasonable deduction should be outright impossible! Now I can't tell you exactly how I know about this *thing* with Vanessa, but I am rock certain about it, and I know that Martin is too. Right, Martin?'

'Yes. It is certainly mystifying but there is really no mistaking it. It is so difficult to explain. Let me try though. We were in each other's minds and we saw Vanessa in yours. Let us say that she was standing outside the door. And we could see her. Now superimpose another image on to Vanessa. It was like looking out of your front door and seeing an army of *millions*; not two or three more soldiers but millions of fully armed combat troops. It was awesome! That's an overused word, but it really was. Now, that is just a metaphor of course, I did not *actually* see any soldiers, I just sensed the firepower there. Crazy as this sounds, I do not think there is anything that could stand against your twin minds if they were conjoined in the right manner. I used to be a chemist. Put the right innocuous elements together and POW, watch out!'

Corvette said 'Properties of the mind are a largely unexplored region. No limits have been defined.'

Rio said 'Well, as I said earlier, K and Corvette are smart ladies. If you do not rule it out then, whacky as it sounds, I will try to keep an open mind. But I think there must be more to it.'

Clovis said 'I liked the example of millions of troops outside the door but if you will allow me the last word on this, I think I can explain what I sensed with Vanessa occupying the same space as Rio. It was off the scale, like a dam holding back trillions of gallons of water. But not water. It was more like raw undiluted energy. And we should leave it at that I think. It's time for a pot of coffee.'

As Clovis moved to organize a brew, there was an almighty piercing scream. Several of the Jeebers were trying to restrain a frenzied man who had stabbed a neighbour in the arm and was flailing around like a man possessed. Worse, other Jeebers were succumbing to the pressure of external minds. The enemy had found them and were penetrating their defences as easily as the wind blows through leaves. Rio sensed Martin thinking that the slaughter would be over in just moments but at the same time she felt his anger and outright hatred of the enemy building like a furnace inside of him. He was thinking of his son and D, L and M, and the other girls that the enemy had slaughtered. Incandescent with rage his mind surged toward the enemy and Rio followed him somehow to what seemed like a wall of total darkness. Then she saw that darkness comprised indiscriminate shapes that were visible only because they were even darker than the blackness that surrounded them. She felt pure malice emanating from them. Without knowing how she was doing it, she began to trace back those vile lines of thought that were infecting the occupants of the room with gut wrenching hatred and violence. She lurched suddenly, as one of the enemy attempted to lock onto her mind. She felt it seize her, and try to inject her with a sort of poison of the mind. It was brutalizing her with images of atrocities. At the same time, she felt her whole body burning.

She screamed and kicked out with her mind and broke the enemy's lock on her. Then she reached out with her mind to Clovis and Martin drawing them to her. Rio seized upon Martin's immense anger and Clovis' determination and she funnelled raw energy into the channel they had created. The result was astonishing. Rio sent an incandescent tidal wave straight at the darkness. The result was an explosion that created light as radiant as that of the sun. The thin membrane over biological eyes could not possibly have withstood it. But this was the light of the mind. It was the energy of thought, directed as narrowly as a laser beam into the heart of the enemy. The beam comprised Ultra-waves, and they cause whatever they reach, to oscillate at a companion frequency. But there is nothing that oscillates at that frequency, or anything close, so the atoms just fly apart. The enemy was gone; completely obliterated without trace. Martin, Rio and Clovis looked at each other in disbelief but just as they started to breathe again they all sensed something at once. Behind the carnage, something else was discernible. Not the enemy, something else; a mind that was even more powerful. Rio could not get a firm reading on the mind that she felt peering at her, but through some sort of veil. For some reason she found herself recalling games in which one has to state, as a clue, if something is animal, vegetable or mineral. This was none of the three, and if there was one emotion that did come across, it was hatred of *living* things.

Rio's vision began to swim. Then, as if releasing a breath that had been held too long, she collapsed.

Chapter 4

Dream-world. Transylvania

MILLIE WAS VERY COLD. There was a thick fog all around, and there was nothing visible through it at all. She looked at her hands. She could not see any hands! No part of her body was visible and neither could she feel anything but the cold. She remembered the moment of her death, that feeling of pain and of wanting to let go. Then a moment of exhilaration when she *did* let go and the pain stopped. What people said was evidently wrong. Her whole life had not flashed before her mind. Her whole life! She had only been seventeen, and now it was done with. And now that it was finished, she could remember all of it clearly; her mother's death; her father as he fell apart; and her aunt who had never recovered either. That was obvious now. Every time her aunt had looked at Millie, she had been reminded of the death of Millie's mother, her sister. She had taken care of Millie despite the pain it had caused her. She had loved her certainly, but it had been hard for her obviously.

Her father had been an additional burden for her aunt. He was a ghost of his former self after Millie's mother died. Then, when he found a way to escape, he took it. He vanished into a dream-world and would have stayed there had Freddy not sought him out. After his return, things had settled down for a while. But then, her father disappeared for a second time. This time though, he had really disappeared. There was no comatose patient lying in a sanatorium. No corpse had ever been found. Maybe he had jumped off a bridge into a river. What difference did it make? He had gone from that moment, and everybody else was left, having suffered so much already. She had never been able to forgive him for that. However much he had been hurting, he had no right to do that to them. And to her!

What would she have done without Freddy? He had become a father to her. Everything her father had not been, Freddy had been. But in the end, even Freddy had let her down. He had not been able to find her father a second time. Probably the fact that there had not been a comatose victim to work with, had prevented him from taking the matter any further. Seekers were not, actually, detectives. They did not search for missing people. Seeking them out in the millions of pathways in their own brains was a different skill set. But Freddy had let her down in another way too. He had left her, just like her father had done. He had chosen to go looking for some stranger in those infernal dream-worlds and he too had chosen other people, over Millie.

Donna was the only person who had really been completely reliable; so clever, so worldly, and always there for her. She had been a true friend. Then something occurred to Millie that gave her a shock. She had done the same thing to Donna! She had managed to get herself pulled into the trap of everlasting sleep. She had left Donna behind. She was as guilty as Freddy and her father. In fact, come to think of it, matters were worse. She had not merely got lost in a dream world, she was actually dead. She would never see any of them again. The realization hit her like an express train. She would never see *any* of the people she loved again! Now, for the first time, she was actually alone! It was too late to tell them how much she loved them. Too late even to say goodbye. So, what had been the point of it?

'Are we dead?' came a voice from behind her. Millie's heart leapt. It was Vanessa. Never had she had such an insight into the difference that just one person could make. So long as there were two people in the universe, a person was not alone. And heavens, how much that mattered! No matter how bad things got, sharing the experience was fundamental. And apart from that, it was such a joy being reunited with Vanessa.

Vanessa answered her own question. 'I don't think we are.' she said. 'Can you see me?'

'No.' Millie answered.

'Well that does not bode so well then!' A second later there was a howling sound in the distance.

'Was that a wolf?' asked Millie. 'It sounded like one.'

There was another howl, followed by another. They sounded louder and closer. 'How could they hurt us now?' asked Millie. 'We are dead already. There is nothing of us!'

'That may be' said Vanessa 'but I still think we should get going, over that way, away from where that noise is coming from.'

'Get going how?' asked Millie. 'I am not being funny, but we don't have any legs!' They both laughed.

'We can't be dead.' said Vanessa. The dead don't laugh! Everybody knows that. What's that sound? It sounds like horses?' The fog was beginning to clear.

'*I can see you.*' said Vanessa.

'Yes we're back!' exclaimed Millie. 'Hey!' Out of the darkness ahead, and visible in the fog, was a coach and horses that drew up right beside them. There was no driver! The horses were a black pair, but Millie did not miss that they had red demonic eyes. The coach was black too, with no markings, but the interior was dimly lit and looked comfortable. Since anywhere seemed better than hanging around in cold fog, with wolves approaching, it seemed like the best option to open the door and get in. The interior was beautifully warm and the coach set off immediately.

There was the sound of horses' hooves on what soon became a track of sorts. The fog had thinned to a mist, and under a full moon it appeared like there was forest either side of them. There were still occasional wolf cries.

'Does this seem familiar to you at all? Asked Vanessa.

'*Too* familiar' said Millie.' It is like the start of one of those Dracula movies. I am expecting to arrive at a vampire castle any minute.'

'Yes', said Vanessa 'it does all seem to be a bit of a cliché.'

Millie said 'Well here is a brain-teaser then. If we are dead, and the vampires are *undead*, then who is the most alive, them or us?'

Vanessa said, 'I have to admit I am well out of my depth with this but I will tell you what: Compared to being just dead and cold in the fog, without a body, I would take a warm coach any time, no matter where it leads.'

'Yes, anything is better than being killed by snakes.' said Millie making movements with her hand and hissing. To their astonishment, having been reunited, they were both feeling really rather high. But they were not sure whether a celebration was in order when, moments later, they were proved entirely right. The coach came to a halt in front of a dark gothic castle. The horses waited patiently for the young ladies to alight but they hesitated.

'The last time we took a risk it did not go well' said Vanessa eyeing a large black door under the porch that did not look particularly inviting. Nevertheless, since a return journey to wherever that cold foggy spot had been, was not attractive either, they disembarked. The coach departed immediately, leaving but one option. Vanessa knocked the door with her bare fist. There seemed to be no door-knocker. It did not do the trick because there was no answer. She looked at Millie, who nodded her a *do it again* signal. This time the door opened slowly. An elderly grey gentleman stood barring their way with a dull reddish light behind him. He was dressed in a smart black suit and white shirt with bow tie. 'Yes?' he said, seeming quite surprised to see them.

'Hello,' said Vanessa. A carriage brought us here!'

'Here?' said the man. 'We do not have visitors here.' His expression suggested that the conversation had ended and he moved to close the door on them.

'Please' said Millie. 'We are lost and do not know where we are. Could we, I mean, do you have something we could use, borrow, to call someone?'

The man looked confused.

'You had better come in,' he said. 'I think this is something the Count will want to deal with.' Millie shot Vanessa a look.

'The Count?' she said as the man stood aside and let them walk past him cautiously. The hall was exactly as expected. The walls were decorated with animal heads including dear, foxes, wild boar, and even the head of a black bear.

'My name is Karlic', said the man. 'I am the butler. I will show you to your rooms.'

"Our rooms?' said Vanessa. We weren't expecting, that is, we would not want to impose...'

"Nonsense' said Karlic. It is far too late to reach the village now. The Count enjoys a late dinner and, although we are not used to company, we have not completely forgotten how to extend hospitality.' He led the way into a very large room with a dining table in the middle that, despite the vaunted lack of guests, looked as though thirty people could have dined around it quite comfortably. A large staircase lay beyond it. Karlic paused to light a small black candle that seemed quite inadequate, and led the way upstairs. At the top of the balcony they turned right, then right again. After that, there was a small spiral staircase that led to the floor above. There were perhaps four more turns until Karlic said to Vanessa, 'This is your room. A fire has been lit for you. I do hope you will be comfortable.'

'A fire lit for *me*?' said Vanessa a tad hastily, and with something between alarm and consternation in her voice.

'Yes' said Karlic. It gets awfully cold in the castle at night. There are thick blankets too. I think you will find it very cosy.'

Vanessa was framing a question in her mind. She did not want to sound ungrateful or suspicious, but a few moments ago, this man had been surprised to see them, and now, apparently, there were rooms made up for them with ready-made fires burning! But before she could say another word, Karlic turned to Millie and said, 'Now if you will follow me, I will show....'

'Could we not stay together?' Millie half exploded, indicating Vanessa. 'Share a room, I mean.'

'Well, there is only one bed', said Karlic. 'It is large, but we do have plenty of other rooms and....'

'No, really' said Vanessa. 'We really *do* like to be together. We were separated for a while and we have been through some pretty awful things to be honest. We would feel much more comfortable together.'

'Very well. The fire may need a bit of stoking, when you come back to the room.'

'Come back?' said Millie.

'Why yes, when you return after dinner. Once you have made yourselves comfortable, the Count would be honoured to have you for dinner. You do remember the way?' Neither looked at all confident.

'Good. Shall we say twenty minutes then?' He turned and left. Then he stopped and turned again. 'I should have mentioned that the bathroom is a little way from here and hasn't been pre-warmed. You need to head further down this corridor, then take a left and follow that corridor along until you reach a little atrium with trophies. Cross the atrium and the bathroom is right there in the next corridor on the second right. You can't miss it. Take a candle with you because it may be dark. Now, if you will kindly excuse me.'

Closing the door, Vanessa said 'This is really too much! All that way in the dark. Well nobody will be making that journey alone!'

Millie said 'No, they will not! I told you. And did you hear what he said? The Count wanted to *have us for dinner*. Drink our blood is what he means. This is a vampire castle. It can't be anything else. We have to escape from here.'

'I entirely agree that that is what we need to do. But escape how? With what? We don't have transport. And to where? We don't know where we are, where to go, or how to get there! Speaking for myself, I do not consider tramping through a black forest, with wolves and no sense of direction, a practical alternative.'

'Well, when you put it like that,' said Millie. 'Oh Vanessa, I am so glad you are here' and she threw her arms around her. They stood just holding each other for a little while. Then Millie said 'Do you think that vampires really do exist?'

Vanessa answered 'At this moment. I am not absolutely sure that even you and I exist! I don't know what to believe!' There was another wolf-howl. Millie walked across to the window. 'You're not going to believe what we have tonight' she said.

'A full moon, perchance?'

'Of course. You got it in one.'

There was a much louder wolf-howl and Millie jumped, and shot away from the window and took Vanessa's hand again.

Vanessa said 'Don't forget we already died once. I don't feel any effects from the snake poison, and look, no bite marks! Wherever we are, we heal fast here. But then both ladies jumped together, as this time, it seemed the window had nearly blown in, following a massive tidal wave of wind that that crashed into the building.

'It is good to have a castle around us, with weather like that!' said Millie.

Vanessa replied 'I may be wrong, but I shouldn't think that camping is very popular in these parts, what with the weather, and the other things roaming around out there.' The absurdity of it all hit them simultaneously, and they both burst out laughing.

After a while, it was time to brave an audience with the Count. To their relief, taking half a dozen wrong turns, being confused by the routing instructions Karlick had given them to the bathroom, they eventually found their way back to the dining hall. Several places were laid out, but nobody else was there. As they reached the table, which was decorated by a white candle centrepiece, Karlic appeared, and showed them to their seats. They were seated together, and after all the wrong turns in the castle, had built up quite an appetite despite their unsteady nerves.

Please excuse the Count not being here to greet you,' Karlic said 'he has been delayed in the crypt.'

"Delayed in the crypt!' squeaked Millie, pressing Vanessa's hand.

'Yes indeed, but all is well, and, ah! Here he comes now!'

The Count approached them from an alcove situated behind them. He certainly looked the part, right down to the black cloak that he gathered up expertly before seating himself at the head of the table, close to his guests.

'I bid you a good evening' he said in a faintly Romanian accent' and I welcome you to Castle Vlad.'

Millie sat up. 'Vlad,' she said.'That is the name of this castle?'

'Yes indeed.' said the Count. And he beckoned to Karlic to pour drinks. 'I hope *Palinka* is to your liking' he said. 'It is a traditional libation for us.' Vanessa took a sip and looked at Millie. 'It's brandy.' she said.

The Count said 'A type of brandy yes, made up of various fruits.'

'It is very warming', said Vanessa. The Count almost smiled. 'That is very much the point' he said. Millie took a sip. She didn't much care for it but she said 'Yes it is very warming. Can I ask you a question Count? How long have you lived here?'

The Count looked thoughtful. 'Well the castle has been part of our family estate since it was built in the Twelfth Century. It was on higher ground back then. We have had steady subsidence over the centuries you know, but when it was first built, and only from the highest tower, there was a view of the river Danube. In those days, it really did look blue when the light caught it on certain days. It was like a deep blue necklace in sea of green. Quite lovely.'

The Count was describing the centuries old view as though he were speaking from personal experience, which only lent credence to Millie's suspicions. But before she pushed the matter any further, she caught Vanessa's expression, and saw an almost imperceptible shaking of her head. She decided it might be better not to know, and gave the Count a big smile to convey her delight at such a charming dinner story.

Whatever else might have been in play, there could be no faulting the hospitality thus far. Indeed, Karlic, who had slipped away quietly, now returned with steaming bowls of hot food that he laid before them, with a hint of pride in his expression.

'Ah' said the Count 'How precipitous. You have come on a *gulyas* night. It is another of our traditions.' The food proved to be outstanding.

'Hungarian ghoulash!' said Millie. 'Delicious.' Millie and Vanessa exchanged glances. It seemed like a lifetime since they had tasted hot food. Perhaps it had been!

The Count used his spoon slowly, until Vanessa noticed that he wasn't actually eating anything. The Count's bowl remained full until the ladies had demolished theirs, leaving empty bowls.

'Well, what a lovely evening!' said the Count as he got to his feet. 'I wish you a pleasant night, and Karlic will show you to your rooms when you are ready to retire. You will want to meet my sons, of course.' And he glided away towards the least well lit part of the hall, and gave the illusion – if that is what it was – of just disappearing.

'His sons! said Millie. 'Remember the sons of Dracula! Oh, my God!'

Vanessa said 'Pass me more of that brandy; or should I be keeping a clear head? Yes, on second thoughts, no more brandy.'

'Oh, that would be a pity. *Palinka* is perfect for this occasion.' Two incredibly tall dark handsome men approached the table, silently, with such poise. They too were dressed smartly in suits and bow-ties. There was something else that was immediately obvious. They were twins.

'Good evening; said the first. 'Excuse us, we ate dinner earlier. My name is Yusi'.

'And mine is Lenta' said the other, while Karlic was filling all the glasses. 'Charmed.'

Karlic said 'Will that be all for the evening, Gentlemen?'

'Yes, thank you, and goodnight' said Yusi. 'That will be all. We will show the ladies to their rooms in due time.' Again, the ladies exchanged glances.

'Shall we adjourn to the Drawing Room?' asked Lenta, already getting up, as was Yusi.

The adjoining Drawing Room was very pleasant. It had a large log fire with a black sheepskin rug in front of it. The walls were hung with large oil paintings, presumably of previous members of the household. Above the fireplace, there was a picture engraved into the wall, of a woman leaning against a large sword. Standing just a little behind her, was a robed friar, with no face. There was something compelling about it.

'It is so nice to see you' said Yusi. 'It has been a long time'.

'A long time since you had visitors?' said Vanessa.

Lenta said 'A long time waiting for your arrival.' The ladies exchanged glances.

Yusi surprised them by saying 'I imagine you have questions that you would like to ask. Feel free.'

Vanessa said. 'Well, firstly it would be good to know where we are, apart from the obvious that we are in a castle redolent of vampire myths.'

'Very good' answered Yusi. 'And you think this setting is unreal?'

Vanessa continued. Well, I do *not* think that you are vampires and, yes. I think this whole place is some sort of contrivance, like a sort of movie set.'

'Well, there you would be wrong' said Lenta. 'In fact, this place is the most real of any places. It is a contrivance in so far as it may be a familiar setting drawn from your own minds, but the place itself is as real as reality gets. It is, in fact, a place between places. Think of it as a crossroads or, if you like, a bridge.'

'A bridge between the living and the dead?' asked Millie.

Lenta smiled. 'No. That is not it. No. It is actually a meeting place between substance and form. That is, between the way things really are, and the way they *seem* to be.'

These words were generating more questions than answers. Vanessa had come to learn that words often failed to convey the facts and truth of the matter. She reached out instinctively with her mind towards the twin brothers, probing for answers.

'That will not work here.' said Lenta. 'You must have noticed that we do not have those kinds of connections here. Our thoughts are our own, and nobody is more special than anyone else. That is one of the key differences about this place.'

Millie said 'I have a question. What's in the crypt?'

Yusi said 'Yes, I suppose it is time. Well, it is not a matter of *what*, so much as *whom*. But before I answer that question, which I promise to do, would you kindly just outline for us how you came to be here?'

Millie and Vanessa took turns relating how they had first met in Capua on the running track and what had happened in Rome. Millie explained that she had only seen Lucius, Lucia and Marcellus fleetingly but Vanessa gave a good account of all that had happened. Yusi and Lenta remained quiet until Vanessa mentioned Varus and his recent mental disintegration, and his transformation, culminating in his dramatic disappearance from his balcony.

Lenta said to Vanessa 'Did you have any contact or sense of Varus at all yourself?'

'Not directly,' replied Vanessa 'but I did sense him second-hand as Lucia and Lucius were talking about him. I sensed Varus in Lucia's mind. It was horrible; indescribable. I was left in no doubt that what Lucius and Lucia had said about their father, was true. His mind was staggeringly powerful, or rather, the mind that was possessing him was. It was evil.'

'Evil is a term we avoid using.' Yusi said. 'It is an imprecise term and one that is very subjective. It is often used as a propaganda term like "monster." Quite often, it has been the case that so called "evil monsters" were, in reality, victims of some trauma themselves that, in turn, led to them becoming unbalanced and not entirely responsible for their actions'.

Vanessa said 'Well that might be an enlightened view, but a contentious one. Nevertheless, that was pretty much what Lucia was saying about Varus. She seemed convinced that he has been taken over by something altogether alien and bent on vengeful destruction. Lucius and Lucia both seemed to think that there might be a way of defending against Varus' possessed mind by – well this will sound crazy – by, sort of, combining mental strengths of suitable people, although I am not sure how.'

'By "suitable people" you are referring to the likes of you and your sister I presume?' said Yusi. 'Not that there are any more people anywhere like you and your sister.'

Vanessa replied with a troubled expression 'I did not mention that I had a sister. I thought you said that talking without words was not possible here?'

'It isn't' said Lenta. But some things are so indelibly stamped and impossible to miss. And in case you hadn't noticed, twins are rather perceptive when it comes to recognizing other twins. 'It is, as some are fond of saying, *just one of those things.*'

There was quite a long silence. Then Millie said, 'So are you going to tell us about the crypt?'

Yusi looked uncomfortable. He replied 'I am. But you are going to find out for yourselves quite soon. We have a prisoner in the crypt.'

'A prisoner!' exclaimed Millie.

'Yes' Yusi continued. As I mentioned, this is a special place. In practice, what that means is that, even the most extra-ordinary minds, have no potency here. Strength of will, and the other stuff of the mind, that creates the sort of power that Vanessa just described, do not operate here. That means that if Varus were here, he could *not* influence anything or anyone with his mind. Now we said earlier that we do not use the word "evil", but in the case of our prisoner, I think any rational person would be prepared to make an exception. Neither would the term "monster" be out of place. Before I say more about him, there is something that needs to be understood. Throughout history, the human species has always believed in some personification of evil. Even in civilizations that had no belief in God or gods, there was invariably some kind of entity that embodied evil, and was a source of fear and control in societies. Can you guess at why?'

Millie said 'Is it because it is true? Is there an entity that embodies evil?'

Lenta said 'Certainly there is, but possibly not in the way that you have been taught to believe. And it is important to recognize the difference between belief and faith.'

'Don't they amount to pretty much the same thing?' asked Vanessa.

'No' said Yusi.

Lenta continued. 'That is a popular misconception. Belief arises when one has accepted a set of facts to support that belief. Faith is a belief that is not supported by facts or evidence. As a result, no facts or evidence presented can be capable of dislodging it. Belief can be simulated. Faith cannot. One might say that the two things are made up of quite different materials.'

Vanessa and Millie just looked at each other.

Vanessa said, 'I was hoping for some answers here, but I am not sure that things are any clearer!'

Lenta said 'I sympathize, believe me. But not every question has an answer. I do not mean that we do not know the answer. I mean there literally really is *no* answer to some questions. Things would be easier for you if you could grasp that.'

Millie said, 'That sounds like a cop-out'.

Lenta replied 'I do understand what you mean, but let me give you an example of a very simple question to which there is absolutely no answer. Can you guess what the question might be?'

'*Is there a God*?' said Vanessa.

Yusi replied 'That is an esoteric question that falls into the *faith* category that I was describing earlier. I am talking about a question that you can deduce objectively and scientifically has *no* answer. There was silence. 'No? You will kick yourselves when I tell you. OK. 'What came first, the chicken or the egg?'

'Oh, come on' said Millie that's not fair. It's a cliché. Everybody knows that one!'

'Yes', said Yusi 'Everybody knows the question, but which of all our learned forbears has provided the answer? Socrates? Plato? Aristotle? Nietzsche? Darwin? Kant? Marx? Satre? Plenty of time has elapsed to solve the mystery. Pause and think about it a moment and tell me, what then is the answer? Think of it on a larger scale. What comes first, the ostrich or the egg?'

Vanessa said 'OK, I take your point. Some questions have no answers. Are you saying then that there is no answer to what Millie asked about the source of evil?'

'No', said Yusi, 'that is not quite what she asked. What you call evil, is the shadow of man himself. There is no atrocity so bad that human beings have not committed it. There is nothing that an alien, or evil god, or devil could do to you, that has not been done to people by other people. Whether it be extermination camps with gas chambers, or mass torture or anything you can imagine; it has been done by one human being, to another. Countless people are harmed in their own homes by their own families. There is nothing in anyone's darkest nightmare that can trump reality. The demon is in ourselves. We carry the sickness ourselves.'

Lenta added 'The point is that the prisoner we hold is the dark shadow of our own horrors. He is the personification, the embodiment, of everything we fear, and everything that we ourselves have created. Here, alone in all creation, his insane mind is contained. He is asleep, but his mind is so powerful that his dreams flood every stream of consciousness. It is his dreams that have been felt contaminating human history, and have inspired countless mythologies about gods and demons, and tacitly sanctioned the darkest chapters in our combined histories. The prisoner is the embodiment of the horror in our own make-up, reflected in a dark mirror. It is not known what would happen if he were to wake up, but that is a question that we certainly would *not* want answered. And now you must meet him.'

'Meet him!' Millie almost shrieked. 'You are joking!'

Lenta said 'Not you Millie. It is Vanessa that must do it.' He looked at Vanessa. 'It is what you came here for. You have to enter his presence and engage his mind. You want to help your friends in Rome and elsewhere, yes? I must tell you that you are still too weak. The only way to develop the strength you will need is to align your mind with that of the prisoner. It is *you* who must be the vampire, sucking from his mind. If you survive the encounter, and I truly believe you will, you will emerge a thousand times stronger. Surely you do not believe that you are here by coincidence?'

Vanessa said 'This is crazy! What if he were to wake up?'

Lenta smiled 'You have a remarkable mind, you really do' he said to Vanessa 'but standing alone and pitting your mind against the prisoner would be like tossing a candle into the sun. He will *not* be conscious of you. But you can draw from his strength. I invite you to think of the way that a tennis player improves his game by playing a better player. Or the way a boxer trains by trading punches. Even the strongest athlete needs to train.'

'And what about me? said Millie, feeling somewhat outshone, 'Do I not get to improve my mind?'

Lenta said 'You are by no means strong enough to be taken that close. Minds have different qualities and yours is fitted to a quite different purpose. Trust me Millie, your part in the story ahead is pivotal, but you are not part of the heavy artillery, as it were. Your qualities are greatly appreciated in a manner that I am not at liberty to explain at present.'

Millie was not deterred. 'I want to go with Vanessa and stand beside her.' she said.

Yusi replied 'You can go as far as the entrance to the crypt, but Vanessa must enter alone. Your mind would stand no chance to survive it Millie, and you cannot be risked. Lenta and I cannot enter either. Vanessa must be alone. Only her sister could have entered with her, had she been here. On the other hand, that combination would have certainly woken up our prisoner, and we are not ready for such a confrontation at this time. No, things are moving, as they should move.'

Vanessa said 'Out of interest, what about the Count? He was in the crypt earlier according to Karlic. Where does he fit into all this?'

Lenta said 'He is the one keeping the prisoner asleep! You cannot begin to imagine how much of a toll that takes. The Count is entirely unique. Our father's mind can generate Theta waves that flood the crypt in a dampening field, like a massive general anaesthetic.'

'I don't understand this.' said Millie. 'If the Count has been in the crypt and he is keeping the prisoner asleep with this Theta field, then why can't the Count go in with Vanessa. You said her sister could. Why not the Count?'

Yusi looked at Millie. 'I can see why any rational being would be fond of you, Millie. You have such spirit, and you fight for your friends. You don't give up, do you? Let me put it like this. Every face is different. Every thumb-print is different. Every signature is different.

Now - every mind is different also. Some minds fit together in a way that fits. Vanessa and her sister, Rio, for example, they fit. In fact, they fit like nobody else ever has, or ever will. The Count's mind is unique – but it doesn't fit with Vanessa's mind. The Count's mind does not fit with anybody else's. That is what *unique* means, and that is just the way it is. Now, really it is time. Shall we go?'

Chapter 5

Dream-world. Nevada

MARK MOORE WAS THINKING: Could there be any more of a cliché than motoring to Vegas in a pink open-top Cadillac? He was seated next to Rhea in the back, and turning to admire her long copper hair flying behind her. She was truly a beautiful woman, even if she did have the knack of speaking in riddles. Freddy was up front, driving. They were taking turns.

Mark was saying 'I hope Rio and Vanessa are OK.

Rhea said 'You like to say "OK" a lot. Do you know where the term comes from?' Mark shook his head.

'Well, the eighth President of the United States, Martin Van Buren, was born and raised in the New York town of Kinderhook and he developed the nickname "Old Kinderhook." It was shortened to "OK" as election supporters formed "OK clubs" around the Country. Van Buren's influence cemented the term OK. But it was first introduced into the vernacular in a low-key manner having appeared in an article in the Boston Morning Post as a shortening of an ironic misspelling "oll korrect." So now when you say "OK", you are in the picture! And if you keep saying it, I will give you another lecture!'

Freddy called out 'Sorry to interrupt the interesting *tit-bit hour* but we have problems.' He stopped the car abruptly and said, 'Look at those!' In the sky ahead was a large flock of what looked, at that distance, like giant birds. 'Pterodactyls' said Rhea. 'They would tear through us like paper.'

They were already sweeping towards them.

'They are here because of me' said Rhea.' I am attracting unwanted attention. You two are going to have to get to Vegas without me.'

'Where in Vegas?' asked Mark. 'We do not know precisely where we are going.'

'I think I do.' said Freddy. Mark was about to follow up, but was stopped abruptly in his tracks. Rhea was gone.

Mark recovered. 'I hope you *do* know' he said 'because our guide has just *vanished* into thin air. It seems anything goes here.' Freddy had turned the car around, and had his foot to the floor, but the pterodactyls were still closing fast. The first overtook them with ease, screeching as it passed closely overhead, quickly followed by close fly-bys either side. The car skidded off the road on to a dirt path that went off at a right-angle to the road. There was some sort of building ahead. A giant claw descended into the seat right next to Mark and he leaned over far to the right, as if the beast would be discouraged by such a nifty tactic. There was the unmistakable sound of shots coming from ahead. A small group of soldiers had emerged, and had opened fire on the flying aggressors. One gave a mighty shriek and peeled off. But others did not seem deterred. Freddy brought the car to a screeching halt to the side of the oddly shaped building, and he and Mark sprang through an open doorway. The soldiers, one of whom had been wounded, piled rapidly inside behind them. There was an almighty crash and the whole edifice shook, denoting that one of the creatures had flown into the building, perhaps in a kamikaze action.

'Down here quickly' shouted one of the men. Mark and Freddy stepped downwards on to what appeared to be a descending series of platforms, or a staircase that would have looked perfect in the "Land of the Giants." There was a massive thud, as a huge steel door closed above them.

'Unless I am very much mistaken,' said Freddy, 'we are in a nuclear bunker.' There was now, literally, no sound from the outside. The door that had evidently been constructed to withstand a nuclear blast, was the perfect antidote to flying dinosaurs.

Mark said, 'Did you know this was here?'

Freddy replied 'No, but I felt sure that Rhea would not just have left us to fend for ourselves without a contingency plan. As a matter of fact, I am not entirely sure that she had not foreseen all of this, and planned in some contingencies. I mean, a bunker, right here, when almost nothing else could have protected us!'

'Who did you say Rhea was in Greek mythology? asked Mark

Freddy said 'Well we can talk about it later, but the short version is that she was the wife of Cronos, and the mother of Zeus, Poseidon and Hades. She was a Titan.'

'Gentlemen would you come with me please' said a young officer, as he extended his hand in the direction of travel.

They were escorted to a small office and greeted by a senior officer. 'I am Colonel Moore' he said indicating a seat for each of them. Then he addressed a corporal standing by the door. 'Bring these men some coffee.'

Mark said 'We have a coincidence, Colonel. I am a Moore too. Mark Moore.'

'And I am Freddy Fox. Sorry to have descended on you unannounced like this!'

Colonel Moore said 'Well these are very strange times. A little while ago I would have been astounded at the prospect of dinosaurs flying around out there, but after all the crazy things going on these last few weeks, hell, now it wouldn't surprise me if a giant alligator were to appear and sing the stars and stripes! At first I thought I was dreamin' but it just kept goin' on an' on – well, here we are.'

'And where is that?' asked Mark.

'Where? Utah. Salt Lake. One of my officers here is a direct ancestor of the Shoshone. Mind you, back in the day, the church encouraged polygamy here so tracing your ancestry ain't entirely an exact science if you get my drift. Anyway, where'r you boys headed in that fancy Caddy? I seen it. 'Fraid you're not goin' anywhere in that anymore. It's done.'

Freddy explained that they had been en route to Las Vegas, but had lost their sense of direction. Colonel Moore said 'Well, hell, this must be your lucky day 'cos we got a truck headin' just exactly over there. Assumin' them critters ain't gonna hang around out there lickin' their lips. Or their beaks I suppose I should say! Want a cigar?'

Mark declined but Freddy said 'Actually that would be very nice. I haven't had one for a very long while.'

The Colonel said 'Well 'course you're doin' it in the wrong order, but after your cigar you might wanna get somethin' to eat. Chow here is pretty good.'

Freddy puffed on his cigar and nodded his appreciation. The Colonel said 'I like a man who enjoys a cigar. Says somethin' about his character. Oh, I know all them high handed do-gooders and health freaks wanna ruin just about everythin' worth livin' for, but I don't work my butt off, just to spend my time singin' hymns. I figure a man deserves a few of the good things in life 'afore it's too late?' This time he looked quizzically at Mark.

'Absolutely' said Mark. 'None of us know how long we have. Umm, if it isn't classified, I am curious to know what you've got here. I'm assuming it's nuclear warheads?'

The Colonel smiled. 'Well, I'll tell you the whole thing is *highly* secret. Yep, this whole deal is classified top secret and above. But since I like yer, I'll tell you what we got here: Nothing! Not a damb thing! We are sitting out here, in this Godforsaken hellhole, without a pretty lady for a hundred miles, and without even a shot of whiskey – well not officially anyway! – for I don't know how long, and we are guarding a pile of empty air. Empty air in a box! That's what we got here! And I will tell you, ...Yes?' A soldier had popped his head inside the door.

'The coast is clear, Sir' he said, and saluted.

'Well', said the Colonel, 'I guess that means the truck'l be leavin' soon. Better get that grub in now.'

Freddy said 'Well that is very kind of you Colonel. You have been most hospitable. But I must admit that you have intrigued me now by sharing that you are all here safeguarding an empty space. Surely there must be more to it?'

'Well, there is no more to the empty space, I can tell you that. An empty box is just what it is. As to what it is *claimed* to be by those with overactive imaginations, well that is a different story, and not one I think any man should pay any mind.'

'Has someone claimed that it came from outer space? prompted Mark. 'An alien of some kind, that escaped perhaps?'

The Colonel laughed. 'Hell no! That would have been almost believable.

Mark said 'Maybe we should go back a few steps if you don't mind. When did, whatever they think this is, or was; when did it first come to anyone's attention?'

Colonel Moore looked for a moment, as though he were going to close up and recall that this matter was classified. But he half shrugged and went on 'This used to house ICBMs here back in the day. You know, the Cold War. Then when it thawed, hell they needed to do something with it, so they turned it into a scientific research facility. Now I'm a soldier, not a scientist, and I wasn't here when they were running routines on whatever they were doin'. The military were called in when they made some kind of discovery out of their research. When we came in, we were haulin' this big plastic lookin' box. "Purpose built", that's what they was callin' it. So we hauled it down there and they put the box around the "thing". Or they said they did! Now don't get me wrong when I call it a thing, 'cos you can't actually see it!' It seemed to me at the time, that it was like one of those games we used to play as kids, you know with imaginary guns and holsters, or pretend coffee cups – stuff not really there. Playin', just playin' games.'

'Is it there now?' Freddy asked. 'The box, with the invisible thing in it, that is.'

'Yep,' said the Colonel. According to them scientists workin' down there, whatever they say it is, is still there, 'cordin' to them.

Mark asked 'So, what do they *say* it is, in the box, I mean?

The Colonel looked contemptuous. 'They call it *The Omega* he said. Don't know what they mean by it. Apparently, they have instruments that can tell it is there. Gives off some kind of waves, like radio-waves I suppose; but not regular radiation, that I could understand. Them scientists talk like it spells the end of the world! Anyhow, doesn't ever do nothing; and seems harmless enough to me. Some of the boys have a theory that it is all hokum just so that the Pentagon can keep some big budget line runnin'. I reckon that is the only thing 'round here that makes a lick o' sense.' Anyway, ain't your problem. You need to get goin'. Bye now, and don't be bringin' more dinosaurs 'round here - unless they're invisible! You left it too late for chow now with all your questions.' Now the Colonel looked at them askance. 'You boys ain't pinkos are yer?'

'No' said Mark 'We're red, white and blue, Colonel.'

'And thank you for the cigar, Sir' said Freddy. 'It was lovely to share.' Now the Colonel was completely disarmed. He shouted 'Corporal, take these fine Americans and make room for them at the front of the truck, you hear me?'

'Yes Sir.'

'Bye now. You'all take care.'

Chapter 6

THE TRUCK WAS NOT VERY comfortable but they were, indeed, seated on the front passenger seat, so it could have been worse. The soldier driving was the polar opposite of his Colonel. He could not be coaxed into talking at all. After an hour of a bumpy journey, he did say, out of the blue, that they were approaching Vegas.

Freddy said 'Salt Lake to Vegas in one hour, at thirty miles an hour! Hurrah for random elasticity!'

Mark said, 'So, you know where we are going?'

Freddy replied, 'In a manner of speaking.'

'Boy, what is it with this place? Is there never a straight answer to a straight question?'

'Depends how you define *straight*' Freddy answered with a cheeky smile but continued: 'Seriously Mark, the vague and qualified answers to questions in this environment are a by-product of the environment itself. We are in a changed reality. Rather than having a conversation while physically sitting next to each other, we are communicating directly with one unconscious mind connected to another. How things look, is a simulation. Or rather it is a different type of simulation.'

Mark said 'There you go again! What do you mean *a different type* of simulation? I mean, being awake is real, and dreaming is not real. Well, the dream isn't real anyway. It's very simple. Why do you and Rhea make it more complicated than it is?'

Freddy said 'Those are two separate questions; what do we mean by different simulation? And why do we make it complicated? I'll answer the second question first. We do not make anything more complicated; we simply explain it more fully than most people have the patience for. As to the different simulations that I am referring to, I mean that when I look at you for example I am looking at you in a superficial way. I could perceive you in other ways.'

'OK, shoot, explain what you mean.'

Freddy looked at the soldier to his left. He seemed to be concentrating on the road in with inadequate headlights.

Freddy said 'I can look at you and judge you by your clothes; or by your face or the colour of your skin. If I could see you more holistically I would see your biology. An X- Ray would reveal blood vessels, muscles, organs, skeleton and so on. We are not pretty to look at in that manner. But my eyes do not have the capacity to use X-ray vision. My vision is limited to a very small part of the light spectrum. At the next level down, I could perceive you by your chemical composition and below that by your chemical elements. Below that, I could see you as a collection of molecules, atoms and atomic particles and finally as simple electro-magnetic waves. You are all of these things. The way you look on the surface is a limited representation, or simulation, of what you really are. And those are just the physical elements. There is a lot more to you than just how you look. Fortunately!' he added, looking sideways at Mark.

Martin caught the expression and gave Freddy a mock wilting look in return. 'You sound like just like Rhea.' he said 'but without any of her charm.'

Freddy smiled and said '*Touche*, but that doesn't change the facts.'

Mark said 'Well let me ask you a question that is far from academic. Given the changes going on around us, are we genuinely in danger here. Could those things back there have killed us?'

Freddy replied 'No need to be opaque about that one. Yes, we could be hurt or killed any time. This is a real as it gets, so far as mortal danger is concerned.'

'So, the same applies to Rio and Vanessa?'

'I'm afraid so, yes. But the plain fact, Mark, is that I am not Tarot. Not even close. As a Seeker I worked in defined environments that were, within certain parameters, stable. This is very different. The rules have gone out of the window. I am being forced to question all manner of things. I am beginning to wonder where the dream begins, and ends. Was my life overlooking Central Park real – or was it an elaborate dream? That seemed stable because of its longevity. But lifetimes are relative. All timescales are. The truth is, we have no objective way of judging what is real, and what is not, at any point during our lives. Everything we think we know, comes via electrical signals into our brains. We have no way of knowing, for sure, where they are coming from or whether we are getting a true representation of what lies beyond our senses.'

'I have thought about that', said Mark. All animals have the same number of heartbeats for example. A fly and an elephant have the same number on average, but the lifespan is very different. But does it seem longer to the elephant than the fly? The fly lives faster, that's all.'

Freddy said 'We are back to relative elasticity again', said Freddy. Depending on what we are doing, time passes at a different rate.'

Mark said, 'Speaking of time, we seem to be heading into town.'

The soldier said 'Were here. Over there is the Strip. Where d'you wanna be put down?' Feddy could see a line of small motels. 'Just here would be fine, thank you.'

The Meridian was a modest, blue fronted motel. They didn't have enough money on them for two rooms, so they shared one with two small single beds. 'You take the one by the window', said Mark. 'In case a Tyrannosaurus pokes its head through the window in the night. You are more experienced than I am!'

'Yes, but there is more meat on you' replied Freddy. 'He won't want an old boiler like me. Which reminds me, do you know that chickens are the closest extant relative to the Tyrannosaurus Rex?'

'I had heard it, yes, but I thought it was fake news.'

'Nope. It is backed up by reliable DNA testing. It puts new a spin on the old chestnut with regard to the chicken and the egg. Turns out the *dinosaur* came first.'

'But which came first? said Mark 'The dinosaur or the egg?'

'Exactly', said Freddy. 'We are no further forward.'

Mark said, 'So now we are here, what is our plan for tomorrow?'

'We are looking for a Tarot. Hopefully he is looking for us, or we won't find him.'

'If you say so. You took the window bed. Do you want first or second in the bathroom?'

Chapter 7

Dream-world. Las Vegas

THERE WAS A DINER OPPOSITE the motel. Freddy and Mark headed over for breakfast, and sat opposite each other in a window seat with a first-class view of their motel and the one next to it.

The waitress came over with a pencil behind her ear. She didn't seem to have anything to write on though.

'Take your order boys?'

Mark said 'How about some pancakes?'

'Nope.'

'Alright, how about waffles?'

'No waffles. Got grits.'

'No thank you. How about ham and eggs?'

'Nope.'

'Toast?'

'No.'

Freddy said 'How about coffee? Got any of that?'

'Sure, of course. Two coffees? Fine. We got muffins.'

'Yes, we'll have two portions of muffins please. Lovely.' said Freddy.

As the waitress walked away Mark said, 'I don't like muffins.'

Freddy said 'Well just look at them then. You are always complaining! Enjoy the aesthetic pleasure of their shapes.'

The mention of shapes triggered thoughts of Vanessa and Rio. 'You know,' Mark said 'When I started out with this dream, or whatever it is, I didn't have the sort of control that I was led to believe I would have, but it was still very nice to begin with. You know, relaxing scenery by the bay; *precisely* what I wanted to eat and drink. Not like this! And Vanessa! You should have seen her! Well, you have seen Rio, so I guess you have seen Vanessa too, in a way.'

'Could you really see no difference at all between them?' asked Freddy.

'No'. Not any difference. And their personalities are so similar too, that I would defy anyone to tell which was which.

'Coffee, honey?'

Without looking up Mark said, 'Yes, thank you. You know, I really didn't have very long with Vanessa. Here I am chasing after her and she may well have forgotten all about me by now.'

'Almost certainly.' said Freddy with a glint in his eye. 'But let me ask you this Mark. You say things were *quote* "nice to begin with." But were they more interesting?'

'What are you getting at?' asked Mark.

'Well let me put it this way. You were enticed by a free promotion but the idea was to get customers to buy into a dream, right? Well suppose it had been a movie you had stood in a queue to see. And in that movie a man met a woman, by a nice bay, and they went for a walk, and had a nice time together: would that movie have held your interest? Or even if it did, would you expect it to draw large audiences. I mean nothing goes wrong. It all goes swimmingly. Nobody is in the remotest danger. There is not even a jealousy or intrigue angle. Be honest, would you invest in that movie?

'But that is a movie!'

'Alright then, would you invest in that *life*. That is, a life without challenge; without adrenalin. Without the thrill of the chase, or the satisfaction of winning the game, rather than getting it handed to you on a plate?'

Mark said 'You mean would I prefer a life without pterodactyls trying to kill me?'

'In a way, I suppose I do yes. Was that not surprise and danger in one package? And didn't it make you value being alive while it lasted?'

'I would think the answer to that must be *yes*' said a stranger who had entered by the door behind them. Without waiting to be bidden, he sat down next to Freddy.

'Please let me introduce myself. *Tarot*. I have been looking forward to meeting you both for a very long time.' He called out 'Could I get some coffee here please?'

Freddy said, 'You must be a magician.'

'That I am. And you are friends of Rhea. Any friends of Rhea are friends of mine as the cliché goes.'

'I will not ask you how you found us, said Freddy. Tarot smiled.

'You will go far.' replied Tarot.

'Not too much farther I hope' rebutted Freddy. 'I am feeling saddle-sore already.'

Mark said 'I could make a crude remark here, but I won't!'

Freddy said 'I am somewhat in awe of you Tarot I must say! As a Seeker, I have travelled the dream-paths that you designed more than most have. I take my hat off to you for coming up with such an extra-ordinary invention. I am almost lost for words.'

'Well, that would be a first! said Mark. 'You must be a magician, Tarot, if you can silence Freddy here! But yeah, way to go, man. You have created the ghost ride of the century!'

'I cannot take credit for that', said Tarot. I designed dream-worlds to be safe and free from stress. The idea was to create a sort of theme park where the whole family could enjoy a break from all their troubles. I wanted people to have a chance to relax and heal. But in shooting for paradise, I inadvertently triggered something that I did not anticipate. I crossed a line that, at the time, I did not know was there.'

'I think I am with you', said Freddy. 'Remember Mark when we were talking earlier about how boring life would be without challenges and contrasts. I saw a lot of near paradise locations in dream-worlds in the course of my work. No offence, Tarot, but people got bored in them.'

'No offence taken. You are right. The dream-worlds were imbalanced in favour of harmony and niceness. In making them so safe and wholesome, I quite literally upset the balance in people's minds. I did not realize that we are actually designed to function under stress just as we are under gravity. We need to get sand kicked in our faces sometimes, or we become unbalanced. I tried to sanitize the experiences in our unconscious minds. In so doing, I created a sort of vacuum, and what rushed in to fill it, was black enough to more than compensate. What we are engaged in now is not a battle to destroy evil, like in the comic books, it is to *restore* the balance in our minds consistent with the balance in all things.'

'Oh that's all! said Mark. 'Well, that shouldn't take long. And speaking of taking long, what's happened to your muffins Freddy? I think after all the fuss we had ordering, they have been forgotten!' Freddy quickly gave Tarot the gist of their difficulties ordering breakfast.

Tarot said 'Let me see if I can help. He clicked his fingers.'

The waitress approached immediately and laid two lovely pancakes with lemon and sugar in front of Mark, and ham and eggs with toast for Freddy, piping hot. And coffees refilled all round.

Mark looked aghast at Tarot who merely said 'I have some influence around here. This is my town. So, you parted company with Rhea on the way here?'

Mark said, 'It was more like her parting from us, like, in a blink of an eye.'

Tarot said 'Yes, Rhea is anything but conventional. Other things equal, her consciousness can be in every part of the dream-architecture simultaneously. But they are not equal, which is what we need to discuss. But even before that, you have concerns about your missing friends, some of whom I have had the pleasure of meeting briefly. We should talk a little bit about them first.'

Freddy said, 'Please.'

'Well,' Tarot began 'Millie, Vanessa and Rio are all following their own dream-paths. Ordinarily, I could track them through Rhea, but that would be an absolute disaster at this time.

Mark said 'Why?'

'Because we have an adversary that would pull out all the stops to eradicate them, if it knew that they were connected to me and my plans. It is aware of them, and even some of their mental properties but, having so many things to concentrate upon, it has not joined up the dots.'

'The dots are not joined up for me either,' said Mark.

'Nor me, for that matter.' said Freddy.

'I am afraid that is deliberate.' said Tarot. Sorry to be mysterious, but minds leak, and they can also be probed. What you do not know, cannot be extracted from you. I promise that you will understand everything fully at the right time. I will explain some things back at the house. That is protected to a significant extent. I *can* tell you that, although the ladies are on different dream-paths, they are getting some assistance, or protection you might say. The same is true of Donna, although she is not currently dreaming so to speak.

Freddy said, 'You know of Donna?'

Tarot said 'I met with Donna and Millie along with Geoff the first time that all three entered the architecture. They wouldn't have mentioned it to you because Rhea took steps to scramble the memories of their dream for the reasons I just explained. But the clever bit is, memories rematerialize at the right time. It requires a complex algorithm to manage that when it is being applied for artificial intelligence but, believe me, it is very much more complicated when human intelligence is being "rewired." Any slight miscalculation and massive damage would certainly arise. Fortunately, Rhea is foolproof when it comes to that sort of thing. After I designed her, she helped me rewire *my* brain! But that is another story. Anyway, let us come up for air. Did you have a good trip?'

'I would not call it uneventful', said Freddy. He walked Tarot through the sequence of events from the time they had met up in Greenwich Village to the encounter with Colonel Moore.

Tarot said 'The business with the Omega discovery, raises all sorts of questions. I am not surprised they are keeping it under wraps.'

Mark said, 'Have you any idea then, what its significance is?'

Tarot said 'It would take a long time to explain the potential scenarios. What does Omega mean to you?'

'The last letter in the Greek alphabet', said Freddy.

'There is a biblical reference to *Alpha* being the beginning of things and *Omega* being the end of things' said Mark.

'You are both correct' said Tarot 'but I am not surprised that Colonel Moore did not understand what the scientists were puzzling over. In astronomical terms *Omega* relates to the plane of travel for a body, or to use accurate terminology, in orbital mechanics, it refers to the longitude of the ascending node of an orbit. In mathematics, the omega constant is the unique real number that satisfies the equation. Would you like me to explain that?'

'No!' they both replied.

Tarot continued 'In "sample space" the Omega is used as a symbol of a given set of possible outcomes of the type we were discussing a moment ago. In "statistical mathematics", Omega refers to the number of micro-states in a system. This is important for storing data on the smallest possible hosts. And very significantly, in the quantum realm, Omega represents the Omega baryons that are sub-atomic hadron particles. That is, tiny particles of atoms that differ from Quarks that exist for such a short period of time that they could be said to exist outside of time. This is the definition that interests me the most; particles that both do, and do not, exist. Think of an Oak tree. Now imagine that it existed for a moment and then did not – then existed again! You could only explain it by magic. And yet it is not. It is underpinned by laws *deeper* than known physics. As the good Colonel aptly put it: 'Just a box of nothing!

Mark said 'I am sorry I asked. Tarot, you and Rhea belong together. I didn't understand a word of what you just said! Did you get it Freddy?'

Freddy answered 'I am not entirely sure. I think it boiled down to the point that the Omega could be interpreted in several ways, but they all point to instability and a big ending that is final!'

Tarot said, 'I wish I could summarize as well as you Freddy. That is a skill you have there.'

'Well, that takes the biscuit', said Mark. Freddy, *summarize*!'

Tarot said, 'Well if you gentlemen have finished your breakfast, I would like to invite you home to meet my wife Karen and our tigers.'

'Delighted' said Mark. 'Who doesn't like tigers?'

Chapter 8

The Moon / Dream-world, World's End

DONNA WAS FEELING THE effects of the Champagne as she climbed, fully dressed, into bed. She not only felt light-headed, but also light bodied; not surprisingly. Geoff had accompanied her all the way into her room because she had become unsteady on her feet. He had attributed the Champagne's enhanced affect to "bubbles caused the Moon's low gravity." She lay flat, staring at the ceiling, then called 'Lights out.' She closed her eyes and started to drift. She was being disturbed by a flickering bright light from the window that seemed to be going on and off, at regular intervals. She found it annoying, but could not muster the energy to do anything about it. Just as she started to sleep, the light disturbed her again but, despite the low gravity, she felt heavy. With the light flitting across her eyelids, Donna fell into a deep sleep.

SHE WAS ON A CLIFF overlooking a beach of dark volcanic sand that glistened in the moonlight. There was just the lightest of winds, but the air felt warm and humid. There was a sound of crickets and gentle waves.

Further along the cliff, she could make out the source of the flashing light. Perched on a piece of land that jutted out at the end of a peninsula, was a lighthouse. Donna walked towards it, and another set of lights came into focus. As she approached, she could see a dark young Asian man with impressive muscle tone, juggling fire sticks. He was wearing a patterned sarong, and his skin glistened in the evening light, and glowed when the beam from the lighthouse swept across him. As Donna approached, he watched her, but did not interrupt the rhythm of his juggling. The fire sticks twirled and cavorted above his head. His face looked younger than his body.

'Hello.' Donna said.

'Hi.' he replied and continued his display. The young man seemed to be doing no more than just touching the sticks while they created diverse movements and patterns, seemingly with a will of their own.

'I am Donna.' she said.

'Uh-huh!' replied the young man.

Donna moved her weight from one foot to the other a bit awkwardly, not really sure what to say. He had not volunteered his name. But there was nothing to do but press on.

'Do you live here?' she asked. 'In the lighthouse, maybe.'

'No,' he answered 'I live in Unawatuna, Sri Lanka. But I come here when I sleep.'

'When you sleep?'

'Yes, when I dream, I always come here. Well not always, but most times. Usually, I visit with the old man, over there in the lighthouse, but he has gone away. The last few times I have come, he has not been here, so I practise with these.'

'You are very good; very skilled.' Donna said. So, what do you and the old man talk about when he is here?'

Now the young man collected in his fire sticks one by one, blew them out and laid them down on the ground. 'I do not really talk.' he said. 'You are very pretty.'

'Thank you' said Donna, feeling suddenly bashful.

The young man went on: 'No, he talks, and I listen. In a way, I am his student.'

'So, what does he teach you?' she asked. Now the young man sat down on the soft grass, so she did the same. It was very comfortable.

He said 'He does not teach me in the traditional manner. He is the Master Storyteller. He tells stories, I listen. But I always learn new things from his stories, and I always remember what I have learned. At least, that was how it was. But for some days now the house has been empty, even though the light keeps working.'

Donna said 'I noticed you said he was *the* Master Storyteller not *a* Master Storyteller. Was that deliberate?'

'Certainly, he is THE Master. Nobody knows as many stories as him, or that go back so far. He knows the story of everything. So I have gleaned a lot of knowledge from him, although only a fraction of what he knows.'

Donna decided to make a stab at a question about something that had been much on her mind. She said, 'Has he ever mentioned anything to you about a grouping called "The Architects."

The young man stood up. 'Why do you ask that?' he asked.

Donna suddenly felt rather unsure of herself, as though she might be venturing into territory in which she would not be welcome. She was circumspect with her answer. 'Well, sometimes when I dream, I go to other places too, just like you do. Only a dream I had quite recently was very strange and the term "Architects" came up. I just thought as the Master Storyteller tells so many stories and that he has, you know, so much knowledge, perhaps he had mentioned them?'

The young man replied 'Do you know what this place is called?' Donna shook her head. 'It is called the Lighthouse at World's End. I know that because the Master Storyteller told me an old folk tale or myth about it. He said that, back at the beginning of all things, there had been a small group of designers who agreed to collaborate on a project. At that time, nothing else existed but them. They used their imaginations to fashion things out of materials they created in order to amuse each other. They had different roles. One was a record keeper, so that no knowledge gained was ever lost. One was a pattern-master, who formed patterns out of the newly created materials and designed what later came to be called "symmetry". There were a handful more with different skills and roles. One more was a storyteller. He would tell stories, and the other "architects" as some called them, would bring his stories into being. Then one day everything changed. One of their number breathed life into the stories. The first of the stories that the storyteller told that contained the breath of life was called "The Lighthouse at World's End." That is why the Master Storyteller gave this place its name.'

Donna said 'That is a good story. Thought provoking! Did you ever wonder whether the Master Storyteller and the ancient storyteller were one and the same?'

'I did wonder that, but I never asked. One thing I did learn from all his stories is that there are some things it is better for us not to know. Mystery is part of the reason.'

'Part of the reason for life?' asked Donna.

'No, part of the reason for *everything*.' he answered. 'I have got to go. It is nearly morning and I have to do things. I enjoyed your company and I hope to meet you again. I feel like I know you.' He tucked his sticks under his arm and walked away swiftly. Donna looked at the lighthouse, watching the beam sweep across the water, like a sonar scope. She thought about the strange story. Well it was more like a story within a story. Was it possible that before anything tangible existed there was consciousness? The traditional scientific idea was that matter and energy sprang from a void, life formed from combinations of elements, and consciousness arose out of animal brains. Was it more far-fetched to think of it the other way around?; consciousness first, and the creation of an environment out of which sentient life could evolve? Donna thought of the spacecraft that had transported her to the moon. How long would it take for a series of random events in the cosmos to create something as complicated as that? How much time would have to elapse before every single component was assembled in the correct randomly? And yet, a space-ship was not as complicated at all compared to all creation; not even in comparison to an ant, or even a weed. A weed had life! As Donna looked up, she noticed a second moon emerging from behind the first, a little bit smaller and a little bit brighter. Both moons cast reflections on the water, which the beam from the lighthouse spliced. Just for a second, Donna thought that she saw a dark shape moving up the cliff; or maybe, a shadow. But now it was gone. Then she felt very cold all of a sudden, and the air was sucked away from her suddenly, leaving her gasping for breath. The air was being drawn out to sea, and on the horizon, lit by two moons, was a massive mountain of black water sweeping towards the shore; a black tidal wave. A Tsunami!

Chapter 9

The Moon. Leonov City

'DONNA? DONNA? DONNA can you hear me?' Geoff's voice was resonating close by. Donna sat up in bed, startled to see Geoff bending over her and two others in the room.

'What is it? She said, 'What's happening?' Geoff replied 'We couldn't wake you. Come on, get up. The fire alarm's going.' Now Donna could clearly hear the alarm. She thought of a dressing gown before remembering that she had collapsed on the bed, fully clothed.

'Don't worry about your things.' said a voice coming from a synthetic member of staff behind Geoff. 'Leave everything and just come. Now please!'

Moments later they were scampering along a corridor which, except for them, was empty. Evidently they were the last of the evacuees. One of the characteristics about life on the moon was that "outside" meant something quite different to back home. It really meant just another part of "inside" – that zone still having a pressurized atmosphere. Nevertheless, it was a very large public area that was quite crowded and the hotel staff and guests were huddled in one area. There was an uncomfortable tension prevailing, which manifested in raised voices and pushing and shoving in among the more crowded groups of people. Geoff started to suspect that there was organized agitation going on, as voices got louder and groups of people detached from one group and moved to another, goading and hurling abuse.

Finally, a fight began in a group quite close to where Donna and Geoff were standing. Things got worse very quickly. There were shouts and screams as people were punched or shoved to the ground, some bleeding from wounds to their faces and bodies. With people pushing against them, Geoff put his arms around Donna in an effort to afford her some protection.

There was some chanting of slogans that made no kind of sense to Donna. Then Donna saw a man grabbing Geoff by the neck from behind and pulling him backwards. Donna disengaged from Geoff and swiftly positioned herself behind the assailant. Another man came up from behind Donna and grabbed her around the middle but she elbowed him in the midriff and he crumbled. Then, Donna put her hands over the head of the man holding Geoff and applied pressure to his eyes. He disengaged and fell backwards over Donna who had crouched behind him and allowed his momentum to cause him to fall, slowly, but dramatically to the ground. Now two more men approached, scowling and Donna watched their fists clenching. They both struck out at her simultaneously from slightly different angles but she ducked effortlessly and punched each of them in the groin from her lowered angle. They groaned as they went down, but at that moment, Donna felt someone grab her firmly by the hair, from behind, which had the effect of twisting her around, sideways on to her assailant. Geoff was utterly stunned by what happened next. Donna brought her fist up under his chin with extraordinary speed and the effect was startling. This huge man lifted into the air and kept on going. He must have reached a height of two full metres before he began to descend and then fell into a small group whose backs were turned to him. Whereas a person weighs much less in lunar gravity, their *mass,* of course, remains the same. It was bizarre to see the effect that a man of around two hundred pounds has when falling from a height, albeit relatively slowly, into a party of unsuspecting brawlers. They fell apart like skittles.

But it was not over. Yet one man more attempted to attack Geoff, coming up from behind him. In the poor light, Donna could not quite make out what he had in his hands, but it was potentially something dangerous. In the circumstances, Donna leapt and kicked the man him under the chin. He flew backwards so dramatically that the crowd around them stopped in their tracks to watch. He landed at an awkward angle, unconscious. Ironically, it was Donna who went to his assistance. She lifted him effortlessly, and held him in her arms as she carried him towards a robo-medic which took him from her. Now the fight was gone out of the crowd. They were looking at Donna with surprised expressions. Nobody was more surprised than Geoff. Then a voice called from somewhere way back in the crowd 'Hey, that's Donna! Immediately, people started repeating her name until it became a small chorus. By now, Geoff was very alarmed. He feared that, one way or another, Donna was about to be mobbed. But the effect was the absolute opposite. As her name was shouted all the fighting, as far as they could see, ceased completely. All voices were stilled. It was as if a calming balm had been applied to the entire assembly. Those nearest Geoff and Donna actually took a step back as though it were disrespectful to invade their space. And indeed, many of the faces in crowd, some of which had looked hostile earlier, now had calm, almost awed, expressions. As Donna and Geoff joined those filing back to the hotel following the "all clear" message, Donna could still hear her name being called, but this time it was in low, reverential tones.

Back in the hotel, it became clear that there had been a fire in a guest room that was now extinguished. On the wall screens, around the reception, were depictions of the violent disorders that were spreading on Earth, interspersed with stills of the incoming planet. Donna read the caption. It said: Alarm grows as scientists admit to being puzzled by inability to ascertain velocity of planetary body. The mass of the body is also unknown at this time. Civil unrest and disobedience is growing daily. Evening curfews are in place in many cities and more curfews are expected to be announced tomorrow. Totally unsubstantiated rumours have been spreading that the planet is carrying an army of alien invaders. Many people had reported dreams about massive insects filling the alien planet surface and intending to use human beings as food! Various Heads of State have dismissed these accounts as totally absurd and contrived to fuel disorder as a cover for looting. Looting is taking place in more than one hundred cities on Earth. On the moon, matters are becoming serious too. New Shanghai is under a total curfew as security forces are being pushed to their limits to maintain order.

Geoff said 'It looks like getting to Verne is becoming more and more problematic. This was bad timing.'

'Let's just go upstairs' said Donna. But as they turned to go, somebody else called out her name; then two or three more. As they turned, they saw an image of Donna filling the screens. It was minutes' old footage of Donna holding the injured man in her outstretched arms as she handed him over to the robo-medic. The caption read "Donna rescues the deranged man on the moon who attacked her." It continued "Donna, who was cited by the President of the United States, having discovered the new planet whilst in a coma, today survived a crash landing on the moon. Miraculously, nobody was seriously hurt. Reports are just coming in that, subsequently, whilst defending a friend from an unprovoked attack, Donna used martial arts to disable her attacker and then went to provide the assailant with aid. Many are reporting that Donna's actions, and her presence at the scene, led to a total cessation of violence in the vicinity of Leonov! The Presidents of both China and the United States have urged citizens to follow the example of Donna, and remain calm and sensitive to the needs of others during this unprecedented crisis. President Lee said in an address to the Chinese people just moments ago that Donna had become a symbol for the best in ourselves and an example to us all.

Pretty much everybody present was now standing quietly, looking at Donna.

'Quick. Let's go up.' she said.

Chapter 10

The Hotel on the Moon

BACK UPSTAIRS IN THE small lounge that David had arranged for them, Donna and Geoff just sat looking at each other.

'Alright you go first.' said Donna.

Geoff said 'I hardly know where to start. Well, first then, you never told me you were a kung-fu expert!'

'I'm not.' Said Donna. I mean, I did one year, nearly four years ago, of ju-jitsu at school, but I didn't take it all that seriously.'

Geoff said 'Well you could have fooled me. You looked like an expert out there. You might have remembered some techniques but you showed a lot of strength and you moved like a cat. That is what I would have expected from someone who had been training thoroughly and consistently.'

'Yes, well, that would be the ballet. I only stopped that a couple of months ago and I was a good standard.'

'Well, maybe, yes but all the same.'

Donna said 'Don't underestimate how much strength, agility, speed and stamina that ballet requires, Geoff. You might be surprised. Quite a lot of actors in martial arts movies get the part precisely because they were dancers. The training schedule is punishing I can tell you. If you doubt that a ballet dancer can duck a blow and kick you in the head, then I suggest you sleep on it. Maybe you will get a demonstration in your dreams!'

Geoff said, 'Speaking of which, you gave us a fright back there. I thought when I couldn't wake you up that you had slipped back into another coma!'

Donna brushed her hair back with her hands. 'Not a coma, but I think it was more than an ordinary dream. I think I went into a mini dream-sleep.' She paused and looked at Geoff while taking another sip of lemon tea. 'I met this man' she said, watching Geoff's expression closely. He kept very still. 'I was walking along a cliff top at night, towards this lighthouse and there was an Asian guy there, quite cute actually, juggling fire sticks. Thinking about it, his display was so faultless that it is hard to believe any human could have managed it. I watched the movements as he told me this story about the Light House keeper. It was strangely compelling. It suddenly changed into a nightmare, and there was this huge Tsunami coming out of the darkness. Anyway, it was just a dream.....'

Geoff said 'Perhaps. But what is *not* a dream is all this press attention you are getting. We need to talk about it some more with David, and maybe Gladstone later. I take it we are "up" now? I mean, we are not going back to bed are we?'

Donna replied, 'I bet you say that to all the girls Geoff!'

If Geoff was blushing, it didn't show. He said 'Seriously, Donna. Thank you for what you did out there. I might have been seriously hurt by that maniac. And, I have to say, you did seem to be a calming influence on the crowd. The way some of them were looking at you, well, it was like a Mother Theresa effect.'

Donna laughed 'I assure you Geoff that there is no comparison between Mother Theresa and me. The very idea! The things that lady did, selflessly, day after day, year after year! No, I have been involved in a string of coincidences just as you have been. That's all.'

'Donna, neither of us believes that these have been coincidences. Even I, sceptical, as I am, am coming around to the view that there is a story in play here. And you are part of it; a big part of it actually. I am not saying that I have the faintest idea what is going on but, I don't know. I mean the way things happened out there, was almost like a dream. How do we know for sure that we are not dreaming right now? Who knows what the real world really is? As I said before, we only have our senses to go on, and they can be manipulated. We, in Dreamcorp can manipulate them. What if there is someone more advanced than we are pulling our strings? We might be fast asleep right now!'

Donna said 'I think this is getting to you Geoff. We are in the real world. So is Millie, but her mind is in a dream-world. Everything can be explained including my defensive moves out there. I had some training in the past, I am still fit from ballet and when we were attacked, well, instinct just cut in.'

Geoff said, 'Yes and there we go again with something that we can't explain.'

'What?'

'Instinct. We can't explain it.'

'Yes we can. It's that Darwinian thing. Through the various generations of life, species adapt and instincts are there to provide the necessary information for the young to survive. It's not that hard.'

Geoff said 'That is because you are accepting it like a mantra without giving it deep thought. We can programme a computer with a memory that can be copied across to subsequent generations of computers, we know how that's done. We fully understand the science. Now think of a new-born mammal. It is born with a range of instincts including how and where to feed. It can tap into a memory from before it was born. It can draw from lessons that it never learned. How?'

'Instinct.' said Donna.

'Yes, but don't you see that that is circular! There are things that are in genetic codes. Instinct is not among them, so far as we can tell. Instinct has all the hallmarks of something that has been specifically engineered and programmed in. Not just something that happens after a lot of trial and error. It doesn't add up. It is one of those things that we accept because it just keeps getting repeated. A mother has a strong instinct to protect her child even before she actually has one!

'Well, perhaps we do take certain things on faith without fully understanding them.' said Donna. 'But where does this get us?'

'I am only saying that something as all pervasive and enigmatic as instinct, has all the hallmarks of a supremely intelligent piece of engineering; not something cobbled together randomly out of protoplasmic crud! Darwin's theories work very well with one additional ingredient: a designer for the programme.'

'Or designers,' said Donna. 'Listen, to bring you back to Earth for a minute, or, more aptly, back to the moon, do you think the disruption around here will have prevented them from preparing breakfast?'

Geoff replied, 'I'll call down and ask. I presume we are still meeting David. What time is it?'

'No idea.' said Donna. 'I never know the time.' But a synthetic voice answered 'In four seconds it will be Seven Forty-Two precisely. A buffet breakfast will be served in the "Aldrin" dining room from Eight am. Your guest, David, has left a message that he will meet you there at eight-thirty pm. A table for three has been reserved.'

Geoff gave Donna a parting kiss on the cheek. They looked into each other's eyes for a long moment. Then Geoff got to his feet and said, 'See you there then – Supergirl!' and smiled while holding her gaze. Then he walked towards the door.

'Geoff?'

'Yes?'

She looked awkward. 'No, it's nothing. See you there.

Chapter 11

MARK MOORE WAS EXPERIENCING déjà vu. He remembered beginning a journey in a lovely bay, the one in which he had met Vanessa. He had been staring at the shimmering patterns on the water. Here he was, doing the same again. Only this time he was on a sun-bed around the swimming pool that, along with the Mexican villa that pretty much surrounded it, belonged to Tarot. There were miniature lemon and lime trees at regular intervals around the pool along with flowering cacti of different shapes and sizes and some large earthen-ware pots decorated in colourful designs. Scattered around the pool randomly, were nine white tigers, lazing around and occasionally jumping into the water. As Muna had explained, tigers did not particularly like water, although they were, in fact, very good swimmers. So they just popped in and out, in order to cool down. The Nevada desert air, coupled with the strength of the sun at noon, made its own case for it. And indeed everyone took turns. Karen was in the water at that moment, playing with one of the tigers. It was amazing to see just how quickly a tiger could move in water. Freddy was on a recliner to the left of Mark sipping a cool fruit drink. Muna was lying next to Mark on the other side, blinking contentedly as she stared across the plant filled garden above a dramatic view of the Nevada desert. Tarot was somewhere inside the house, examining the kaleidoscope and catching up on what was going on in other dream-worlds.

The journey from the diner, where he and Freddy had met Tarot, had been the most remarkable of Mark's life. It had left no doubt whatsoever in the mind that Tarot was supremely adept at controlling his own creation. He had paid the bill, and the moment they had stood up to leave, they had just materialized here instantaneously at the Villa! No warning, no strange sensation and no disorientation. They had just gone from one place to another in an instant, as though it were standard practice. When Mark had remarked upon it, Tarot answered that he found journeys pointless, unless there was something new to see.

Mark could not help noticing the similarity between Tarot and Rhea. They often both spoke in riddles, or at the very least, there were cryptic messages that took some deciphering. Perhaps that was hardly surprising. In the first ten minutes of arriving at Tarot's home, Freddy had asked Tarot to elaborate about Rhea and her role in the dream-worlds.

Tarot had explained recounted those early days when Tarot was experimenting with the newly designed dream-technology. Because of the complexity involved, there was no human that he could turn to assist him in his project; nothing less than a super-computer could handle the task. Tarot had needed something capable of fulfilling a batch of quite different needs. He needed artificial intelligence capable of assisting in the concept and design of the dream-architecture. He needed it to be able to handle calculations at a speed that meant it could keep up with *him*; and he needed it be able to take over the dream-architecture and run all the systems required simultaneously. He needed it to be capable of original and independent thought, and of creating other AI entities that were also capable of propagating. Most of all, he wanted a companion that he enjoyed working with, on a long, concentration intense, project. The solution was Rhea. He needed Rhea to be sentient to the same degree as any human, and with the same range of *genuine* emotions. As a result Rhea was the very first artificial life form to feel exactly the same way as humans do. She was the first artificial mind to actually be *alive*. She did not merely comprehend feelings highly advanced processing; she actually *felt* emotion.

However, as Rhea herself had explained when she had met Rio, Mark, and Freddy, in that bizarre garage location by the canal, she had been damaged in the course of eliminating the so called "first virus" nearly two years earlier. The source of that virus remained unknown.

However, although Rhea was Tarot's crowning creation, she was not his first major breakthrough. That honour fell to Muna. As Mark's thoughts turned to what Tarot had relayed about Muna, she nudged him and he automatically stroked the giant cat.

What Mark and Freddy had learned from Tarot was that, although Muna and the other tigers communicated very well, mind to mind, they were feline in nature and preferred to communicate their feelings using body language. Chit-chat they left to others. However, since Muna was Tarot's first AI creation, Tarot had mapped a significant portion of his own brain and grafted them onto Muna's neural pathways. As a result, Muna had a staggeringly high IQ, amongst other things.

Muna and Rhea had assisted Tarot with creating the other tigers and a plethora of other autonomous AI entities that populated the architecture; the *Figs*. They were all sentient and had their own personalities. The Figs were not copies or clones. Nor were they joined up together in a giant computer programme. That would be a total misunderstanding. They could connect at will directly to the Net for information, but they were electro-magnetic individuals. People with a different design specification from humans, but people none the less,

Now Muna stood up, and started nudging Mark. She had taken a real liking to him. She pushed her nose into his chest and started play-biting him. Tarot re-emerged at that moment. He smiled and said 'I see you are all getting along nicely. There is nothing like family!'

Karen had emerged from the pool, flanked by two tigers, tossing the water from her hair. 'Shall we have some lunch?' she asked Nobody was surprised to see a full buffet laid out on a long table behind them. In Tarot's residence, that could quite literally be called a dream home, things happened to order that were indistinguishable from magic.

Chapter 12

Dream-world. Tarot's Home

AS THEY SAT DOWN TO eat, Freddy said 'So, Karen, how about you? We know you met Tarot when he was first developing dream-technology and your wedding was big news at the time, but what is it like living with the great man himself?'

Tarot smiled and nodded at Karen, 'Give them the warts and all version. Go for it!'

Karen said 'Well let's just say that living with Dr Frankenstein is always going to be different. But never dull. There are times, quite a few actually, when I realise that his mind is one hundred percent on his work, leaving zero for me. But when he makes up for it, he really goes to town. He can be romantic, but he needs some encouragement.'

Mark said 'Well, we don't want to pry too much. What about your first experience in a dream-world Karen, if that's not personal?'

'Ah, now that's a good one. I was actually the first person, after Tarot, to go into one. You might say that I was the first actual customer. At that time, the experience was limited to one dreamer at a time. Dream-sharing was not possible in the first phase of the project. So Tarot could not go with me. I had to go alone. I, volunteered! So, Tarot set me up in front of the kaleidoscope, but things were different at that point of development. Although Tarot had the full design specs for dream-ware in his mind, it took some trial and error to actually put it in place and to fine-tune it. At that point, people did not have the option to take control of their dreams but rather just set some parameters. This was before the virus, so it was notionally safe, but one just had much less control. But, of course, dreams are dreams and there is no limit to our imaginations. So, in order to be cautious, I opted to have a gentle walk around a quaint old British village. Sure enough the dream began that way. Then I entered this old-world style bookshop, you know, old hardbacks lined up on shelves and more books along the floor and in every corner. The shop owner was an old fellow with white hair, and he was very softly spoken. He was a major book enthusiast and he took great delight in showing me all these first editions of people like Dickens, Trollope, Chekov, Ibsen – you name it. When I turned to his science fiction shelf, he showed me a book signed by Asimov himself. Then he told me this little story of how the bookshop was going to close down because of high business taxes and not enough customers. He decided that he needed to modernize, to be more competitive in the market of the day.' Karen looked around, to be sure that people were interested.

'Go on.' said Freddy.' Mark was nodding at her too.

'Anyway, he told me that, one day, while moving a bookshelf in the deepest part of the shop, he discovered a small door that he did not know was there. The door was less than three feet high.' Freddy and Mark looked at each other.

Karen continued 'Would you believe that, living in a small room at the back of his shop, was a leprechaun? When the book owner made no fuss, and invited the leprechaun to stay, he had a major change in luck. People started coming in large numbers from great distances to his shop. Along with the rest of the village, it became a major tourist attraction: "The shop with the leprechaun."

Freddy said 'Did you meet the leprechaun? What was his name?'

'Well, he didn't have a name. He said leprechauns had no used for them. But certainly I met him. He was a charming fellow, full of Irish wit and sayings. One of the things he said to me will stay with me forever. He said,

"While you are complaining and feeling sorry for yourself, you could be drinking life in, like the fine vintage that it is! You only get one glass."

Now Karen looked at Tarot. It was not until I was thinking about it later, that the truth of the matter hit me. Some of Tarot's wisdom and love of humanity was embedded in the dream-worlds and the Figs who inhabit them. People who are wandering along those dream-paths are inhabiting the cloned mind of a genius and of someone who cares deeply about this world and all its inhabitants; all creatures great and small. No, Tarot has his faults as we all do. He's the first to admit that he does go on a bit! But nobody has a bigger heart than Tarot; not in my opinion anyway.'

Tarot said 'Well that's quite enough about that.' as Muna dropped her head in his lap.' Suffice to say that my intentions were good. It remains to be seen whether or not posterity judges in my favour. There is all to play for. Now, we should bear in mind that this is Mark's first time in a dream-world. How's it going so far?'

Mark said 'Well, it is a far cry from what I thought it would be. There is certainly plenty of confusion and stress, which is the last thing that I thought I wanted. I am still worried about Vanessa and Rio, but less so since Rhea reassured me that they are not being mistreated as they go about their *quests*, for want of a better word. So, with concern for the twins being my only caveat, as I sit here with you, and reflect on what we have shared, I don't think I have ever been happier. In fact, I will go further, I don't think that I *ever was happy,* before this. Even Freddy has turned out to be *tolerable*!'

Freddy was chuckling.

Karen said 'How about you Freddy? Come on. A Seeker! You must have been in dozens of strange dream-worlds?'

'Yes, more than my fair share probably.'

'Example?' said Mark.

'Well actually, one of the strangest was when I was seeking Roy, Millie's father, the first time he went missing. Basically, after the death of his wife, he had a severe breakdown. That is not the time to go into a dream-world.'

Tarot said 'No, it certainly is not!'

Freddy continued 'Because of his splintered mind, it was difficult to pick up his dream-path. Also, I was new to the job, but he had found himself a dream-scape that suited his frame of mind, but was difficult to reach. I had to walk on water to find him. He told me later that he watched me, for a long time, walking towards him across the sea. Roy was living on a tiny round island no more than eight metres across. You could walk all around it in five seconds! All there was on this island was a coconut tree in the middle, a sun bed for Roy, a jukebox, and an always full ice bucket with cans of beer. That was how he was living. He had no idea how to escape the island and he didn't want to. Mentally, he was unable to cope with anything. That island was an accurate representation of where he actually was, inside his head! He had blocked Millie from entering his mind altogether because, deep down, he was guilty about abandoning her, and it was too painful to think about that, on top of the grief of losing his wife. He was living like a man curled up under a table, covering his head with his hands. He had acute Post Traumatic Stress Disorder. No question!'

Karen said, 'So how did you get him off the island?'

'I created a barely sea-worthy sailing yacht that he had to help sail and keep afloat. It gave him something to do. Initially, he would not engage, but when we were getting soaked in a storm he had little choice. Roy was brought up on an Irish farm. When he gets motivated, he gets things done. We got him back to Millie and we all became close. Now I need to find Millie.'

Tarot said, 'I'm sorry Freddy but that would not the best idea at the moment.'

Freddy said quickly, 'Excuse me?'

'It's the timing, Freddy. Right now, Millie is where we need her to be. I wish I could explain it to you more fully but there are others I want to invite here before I go into it. I am going to ask you to trust me. Rhea is keeping an eye on Millie behind the scenes, as she is with the others. Because of the struggle we are in, Rhea is precluded from acting in exactly the way that she would like, but she is still a formidable ally in any situation and she never loses concentration for one second. There is no better safety protocol in the world than Rhea.'

'I will find Millie for you at the right time.' said Muna.

'You!' exclaimed Freddy.

'Muna said 'Think about it Freddy. I have her digital scent from when we met with Tarot, before the great flood. I have Geoff and Donna's scent too. Once I have someone's scent, I can track them. Moreover, our adversary would not be expecting that. He has neither a feline brain, nor does he think about his nose. He is not the lateral thinker that Tarot is. I will find her and bring her to you safely. Don't worry.'

Tarot said 'If Muna says she can do something, you'd better believe it. I did not design her just for fun. No-one can move along a dream-path faster than Muna. Nothing moves faster than light except something composed of thought. Light moves like a disabled snail, compared to Muna. And her nose is the best precision instrument I know.'

Freddy said 'Alright, I feel somewhat reassured. But I won't relax until I see her.'

Tarot said 'Fair enough. I do want to fill you in on how the others on our team are doing. But I want to bring Donna and Geoff here. We need to have a strategy meeting and, in addition to talking about Millie, I want to put you in the picture about Rio and Vanessa. They are mission critical, and both busy on their own dream-paths at the moment. Rhea is tracking them and lending a hand, in a low-key way, so as not to attract attention from the opposition.'

Mark said, 'I can't imagine seeing Vanessa and Rio at the same time. That would be fantastic.'

'Fantastic is precisely what they are', said Tarot. Even I did not spot their potential at first. They have in their minds something that nobody else has. And I do mean *nobody*. Their minds can generate ultra–waves. Ultra-waves were the building blocks of the universe. There is *nothing* more powerful. Let's wait for the others and I'll explain. There is a beautiful sunset coming up.'

Chapter 13

Dream-world. Dystopia

RIO AWOKE, CHOKING for breath. Martin and Clovis were kneeling either side of her.

'She's alive!' she heard someone shout.

'Give her some water,' said Clovis.

Rio was highly confused. 'What happened?' she asked.

Martin said 'You saved our people. You defeated the enemy. They are gone. Whatever you did, it destroyed them.'

Memories of the struggle were returning to Rio. She remembered the enemy seizing control of some of their Jeeber minds. She also remembered the minds of Clovis and Martin, working together, identifying and engaging the enemy minds. She recalled feeling intensely angry and piling in behind Clovis and Martin with all the force she could muster.

'Help me sit up' she said and scanned the room.

'They're alive.' said Martin. 'All of them.'

'Thanks to you.' said Clovis.

'It was a combined effort. We acted together,' said Rio, gulping back the water.

Clovis said 'Yes it was a three-way effort alright. But it was you, Rio that delivered the payload. I have no way of explaining it, but it is as clear as day to me that your mind is way different from everybody else's; except your sister I think. You can deploy raw energy that is, well, just off the scale. When you focused your mind fully, they didn't stand a chance.'

Martin said 'There was more to it than that. It seemed to me that you reached beyond all of us and drew something from somewhere else. There must have been a thousand hurricanes worth of energy in the blast you delivered - more - and it was aimed so precisely, it made me think of laser targeting sights. Anyway, the enemy is gone. The question is, where do we go from here?'

Clovis said 'We rebuild. We put our lives back together, but this time it will be citizens and Jeebers rebuilding together, and sharing the resources together. We are all human. We change. We adapt. We survive – together. You and I Martin, we can lead the way. After all we have learned, I believe that people will see that this is the only way that it can work. We are not starting from nothing. There is still infrastructure left. Our biggest hurdle is prejudice and suspicion. And if people do not fall in, we will get Rio to give them a firm steer!'

Martin said, 'Inspiring words, and I am right behind you, but I do not think Rio is not intending to stay, are you?'

Rio looked at Clovis and Martin and also at K and Corvette who were sitting quietly listening in.

'I am sorry but my place is elsewhere. So is Martin's. Sorry Martin, but you have to come with me.'

'What? This is my home.' said Martin.

'No, actually it's not', said Rio. You belong elsewhere too, and moreover you are needed. The truth is, I came here to get you. I have a friend, "Rhea", she sent me to find you.

Martin looked very unhappy 'I don't understand' he said 'This has come out of nowhere. I thought you were playing straight with me! I have been inside your mind. You could not have been deceiving me, I would have known it.'

'I wasn't deceiving you' Rio replied. 'I did not know it myself earlier. *Rhea* planted some information in my mind, but left it inactive until the time was right for it to emerge. It just has. It is like, I don't know, like an email just arrived in my head. Not really like that, but that is a way to explain it'.

'Rhea? Who is Rhea?' Clovis asked, with a mixture of consternation and resignation in his voice.

It was K who replied. 'Rhea is our mother. If you think of the architecture of our reality, then Rhea is the nervous system that runs through it. Rhea sustains and nourishes all of us. She is the First Lady. She is in our minds and in the dream-ware in your blood. Rhea is an oracle, and a system controller. Rhea is the consciousness of Tarot's creation.'

Corvette said 'Rio was not deceiving us or holding anything back. Rhea arranges for information to be delivered at the proper time. Since she has the overview, it is redundant to argue about it. Rio is correct, she and Martin need to head to Helius. Clovis must remain and lead the reconstruction.'

Martin and Clovis now had blank expressions.

Rio said 'What is this Helius place?'

'Not a place you would choose to go' answered Clovis. 'It is a unique area; a sort of Free Trade Zone. It is also utterly lawless. A mixture if citizens and Jeebers who were traumatized after the war made it their home. It is highly unsafe and nobody goes there who doesn't have to. That also means we have little news from there and, therefore, not much idea about how life is there now. Of course, there are plenty of rumours and, no doubt, wild exaggerations. We do know that it is the custom there to keep all faces covered. The rumour that prevails about that is that many look deformed and hideous. That is why the inhabitants of Helius are called "the lepers." I think the only way to reach Helius is by the subterranean train. That is if it is still operating. It is too far by any other means. There is a disused pipeline but, if it is not blocked, it would take forever to get there by foot. It would also be very dangerous. That said, the tunnel is not a good option either. The stories about the trains, assuming any could be revived, do not inspire confidence.'

Martin said 'No. Nobody goes to Helius anymore, and certainly not by that awful train. It is a death-trap. Nobody has ever returned from the journey except for the *eye-witnesses*.'

'Here we go again!' said Rio 'And just who are the eye-witnesses?'

Martin continued 'They came back through the tunnel, about six out of one hundred or so of the last batch that attempted to reach Helius. All six returnees were badly wounded. Two died very swiftly. They said that the train had been attacked by the lepers who were, by all accounts, completely insane. Of course, this may be an exaggeration, but they said that they attacked like wild starving banshees in order to – eat!'

'Cannibals, you mean?' said Rio.

'That's what the eye-witnesses said, yes.' said Martin. 'So, whoever this Rhea may be, there is no way that we are going anywhere near that tunnel, nor Helius. That would be insanity!'

'Well, when you express it that way' said Rio 'you do not make it sound all that attractive! But now we have a problem because Rhea is not providing us with any other options.'

Clovis said 'That is as may be. But Martin is right, and gruesome as it sounded, he has also given you a sanitized version. The train coaches are windowless and badly beaten up. Neglect and decay have left them full of holes.' He hesitated again 'There are thousands of rats in the tunnel and they get into the coaches. They carry a potent mixture of plague and rabies.'

'Oh well, of course, they would!' Rio added. 'Next you'll be saying that there are no first-class carriages available! Seriously, I have a thing about rats. My sister, Vanessa, has no problem with them. She had a white one as a pet once, called Patsy. There *are* a few differences between us. I am not going into a carriage with rats. That would appear to leave the pipe as the only option. Obviously, we couldn't walk though. Is there any other way to go through it?'

Chapter 14

Dreamworld. The Crypt.

IT WAS LATE INTO THE night at the Castle. Yusi led the way down the stairs towards the crypt. Vanessa was a step behind Yusi, and Millie followed closely behind Vanessa, trying to suppress the image in her mind of a victim being led to the scaffold.

Yusi and Lenta had said they were confident that Vanessa could survive the encounter with the prisoner, and with her mind not only intact, but strengthened. By way of first impressions, the sons of the Count did not strike Millie as being disingenuous, but she could not set aside the consideration that it was not they, but Vanessa, who was heading to a potential doom. She had a strong urge to reach forward and grab hold of Vanessa and force her back up the stairs. But Lenta was a few steps behind her. Now Millie missed having the link with Vanessa's mind that had become familiar to her very quickly back in Rome. She wanted to send her waves of reassurance.

Vanessa could have benefitted from them. Vanessa felt more and more apprehensive with every step. Her body felt very heavy and she had an image in her mind of standing right at the edge of a totally black pit that dropped away forever, with a knife pressing in the small of her back.

As they reached the door to the crypt, Yusi turned around. Millie slipped her hand in to Vanessa's.

Yusi said to Vanessa 'There are some things that it is important for you to keep in mind. The prisoner is asleep, and will only be partially aware of your presence. The theta-waves of his mind are incredibly strong, but your mind is strong too, in a different way, but still strong. In fact, because your mind operates quite differently from everybody and everything else – except your sister – the prisoner cannot damage you directly and when he brushes your mind you will grow even stronger; that is precisely the point. You will siphon some of his energy without contaminating your mind. However, Vanessa, I will not pretend that this is going to be easy, or pleasant. The prisoner's mind does not contain horrors from another dimension. It houses images that are more difficult to handle and more distressing; the evil that men do. In some ways, his mind is a mirror to the darkest chapters in our history, and even the worst of our everyday life. You will be subjected to a battery of terrible experiences, the worst of which is that, although they are representations, they are the accurate depictions of human behaviour. That will be difficult to take. It will get ugly. Your purity of thought and your innate goodness would not be enough, in itself, to protect you from the psychological damage that this creature could do. Your defence derives from the smallest things in creation; the ultra-waves that occur naturally in your mind. Although there is nothing smaller, there is also nothing stronger by a huge margin. So long as you hold firm to the view that one day these horrors will be relegated to the past, you will cope with it. *Hope* is a massive source of energy. It is the unsung hero of all our successes as a race. One more thing, although we will not be with you and you will feel all alone, you will not be. Nobody is, not even after their last heart-beat. The breath of life is in all creation, even in the blackest void and in the darkest mind. When things get really tough, think of Rio, you may not sense her, but she is tenuously connected to you through the synapses of your unconscious mind. I hope that, one day, the connection will be total, rather than tenuous. That would be something. But for now, we work with what we have. Do you think you are ready?'

'No, I really don't.' said Vanessa. I am petrified to tell you the truth. And I *do* feel alone. I don't want to go in there.'

'Let me go with her; said Millie 'I *insist*. I want to go with her Let me go.'

'No Millie' said Vanessa. 'Really, no. You are not being asked to do it and it's an unnecessary risk. Bless you though. Give me a hug.'

Vanessa took a step into the crypt. The light from the door only penetrated a short way into the crypt. Then a chill ran through her as she heard the door being sealed behind her. After that, all was dark. Vanessa took small steps, trying to will her eyes to adjust to the darkness. As she moved forward, she could just begin to make out a large gothic looking oesophagus adorned with small statues that resembled hideous demons. It was only visible because it glowed very slightly with a dim green light.

Outside the door, Millie was feeling panic. It took all her self-control not to scream, and prize the door open again. But Yusi reached out to her and began steering her upstairs. 'You need to be well aware from here now' he said. 'You can't do anything and being this close is risky.'

Vanessa was feeling very cold. Whereas she was no stranger to feeling cold, this felt colder. In fact, it was a different a feeling altogether It was *deathly* cold.

Now she was at a loss. She was here, but had no idea what was supposed to happen next. How long was she supposed just to stand there? Perhaps if she stretched out and actually touched the tomb, there would be some kind of reaction. But she dreaded a reaction! On the other hand, a person could freeze to death in there. Something had to be made to happen, one way or another. She moved forward in the blackness inch by inch, fingers outstretched until they made contact with the tomb. To her amazement, it was even colder than her surroundings. Still there was nothing; absolute silence. Then unless she was mistaken, she thought she could hear the faint sound of breathing coming from behind her. She couldn't move. Anyway, there was nowhere to move to.

She turned towards the sound of the breathing and towering there, darker than the darkness around it, was the shape of a dark figure. Her pulse was racing and her thoughts were churning ,and one phrase kept repeating in her mind; *Thanatos, the Reaper; Death!*

Vanessa took a step back, utterly terrified. Now she was wedged against the tomb unable to retreat any further. She watched in horror, as the Reaper stretched his arm towards her and she felt his ghostly cold hand passing into her chest. There was no pain. She couldn't move. She felt icy fingertips lightly touching the ventricles of her heart. Then - nothing.

Chapter 15

Dreamworld. Tom the drummer-boy

VANESSA FELT LIKE SHE was lying in cold mud. As her vision adjusted, she found that she was, indeed, lying in a muddy field. The darkness had given way to enough light to make out the vague shapes of men, and there was a scent of gunpowder in the air and the sound of gunfire. The scene before her had all the hallmarks of a battlefield.

Without warning somebody's boot hit her square in the chest and a man tripped over and fell beside her. He was wearing muddy white pantaloons and a red military jacket. He looked at Vanessa with a stunned expression and, despite his fall, he was still grasping his musket in his hands. The sound of musket-fire and canon-fire was becoming deafening. The ground itself was reverberating form nearby canon-fire. Then the soldier turned the musket on Vanessa with the bayonet pointed close to her heart. She closed her eyes and waited for it to find its mark. When it did not, she opened her eyes to see the soldier lying on his back, with a gaping wound to his head. He was dead. Another soldier fell dead right next to him, and a few more, some ten metres away were blown up into the air by canon-fire. Vanessa felt some burns on her face from the explosions. Apart from the sound of the weapons, there was the sound of men screaming as they were hit, some coughing as they choked on the thick black smoke in the early dawn.

'Are you alright? came a voice from above her. 'Give me your hand'. A hand slipped into hers and helped Vanessa to her feet. She felt dizzy and nearly fell back down, but as she reached out with her other hand, it hit something solid. It was a drum.

'It's mine' said the boy who had helped her. His hair was golden blond, almost the same colour as Vanessa's, and he was wearing the uniform of a Redcoat, including white pantaloons. Evidently, he was a drummer boy. He looked no more than twelve years old.

'Are you with Miss Nightingale?' The boy asked.

Vanessa answered 'No, I don't think so. 'Do you mean Florence Nightingale?'

The boy looked unsure. 'Miss Nightingale.' he said.

Vanessa thought quickly. Florence Nightingale was associated with the Crimean war, and the battle going on around here fitted that description pretty well. The priority was to get herself, and the boy, away from the battlefield as quickly as possible. A field hospital would be far preferable.

Vanessa said to the boy, 'Do you think you could help me find Miss Nightingale?' The noise of canon fire had dropped away for a short pause, but had now resumed with a series of renewed volleys. This was no place for her, or a child. The boy let go of her hand, then stooped and wrestled the drum strap over his shoulder. Vanessa said, 'Why not leave the drum?'

'They'll shoot me if I do that.' he replied, and reached for her hand again, and he began guiding her through the mud and swathes of smoke. The fallen were everywhere, and Vanessa could see that the mud all around was saturated with blood. Along with the dead, were a large number of wounded, some crying out in pain, some whimpering, and some choking on smoke. Vanessa remembered Yusi's words that she would see horrors that were depictions of actual human behaviour, and that the scenes were designed to unsettle her. Vanessa could see that some of the dead had been gathered up and formed into large mounds even taller than her. As she passed one of the mounds, Vanessa looked directly into the eyes of a dead soldier who showed no sign of any wound. There was not a trace of blood on him or his uniform. But his vacant eyes stared at her, and his expression was a mixture of anger and bewilderment as though he were asking, 'Why? I don't understand. Why?'

As they walked, a change came over the battlefield; as if by some hidden signal, the artillery bombardment ceased, followed quickly by an end to the musket fire. The boy looked back and said, 'A short ceasefire to make the mounds.' Vanessa was confused by his words, but remained focussed on leaving the battlefield. After a while, the number of combatants and fallen, thinned out, and they traversed an open space. Vanessa could make out an assortment of large tents in the near distance.

As they reached the first tent, the boy took a very firm grip of Vanessa's hand, and pressed on resolutely to the next in line. They approached a marquee with the flap pinned open. The drummer boy led her inside. There were perhaps fifty palettes lying on the ground and every one of them was occupied by a wounded soldier. There were perhaps thirty more wounded men lying on the floor without palettes. Vanessa counted eleven medical orderlies, all male, running around frantically, trying to cope with the wounded. It was hopeless. More of the injured were being helped into the tent at a faster rate than the existing patients could be helped.

Suddenly, the boy darted across the tent and knelt down beside one of the palettes. Vanessa walked across and joined him, kneeling too. The soldier looked no more than around eighteen. His eyes were closed and Vanessa could see that he had been treated for a number of serious wounds. His head kept twitching, but apart from that, there was no other movement. The boy said, 'This is Joey, my friend.'

Vanessa said 'I see. And what is your name?'

'Tom.'

Vanessa was unsure how to continue the conversation. There was a lot of moaning in the room, and Vanessa heard someone close by say 'Can you not give him something for the pain?' Apparently supplies were virtually depleted. Vanessa took another look around the tent. Certainly, there was no sign of Florence Nightingale.

At that moment a blood-stained soldier, walking with the aid of a crutch, stopped next to Vanessa and Tom.

'I think he's the only one left.' said the man said indicating Tom.

Vanessa said 'I don't quite understand what you mean. Sorry.'

The soldier said 'The other drummers were cut down as we marched forward. One by one they fell. He's the only one that survived. He's a brave boy though. Just kept marching and kept drumming. Yes, he's a very brave boy. The rest bought it.'

Vanessa said, 'Maybe some of the other drummer boys are in other tents, wounded but alive.'

'They don't take the drummers in the tents.' said the soldier. 'Only the wounded that can fight again. Only use for drummers is the beginning. They shouldn't put boys and girls in the front line. Just drumming and carrying no weapons.'

'Girls?' said Vanessa. 'They put girls in the front line?'

'Course they do. He's a good boy there.' He turned and slowly walked away.

Then another man approached, with two stripes on his arm. 'Come with me.' he said to Vanessa. She stood up and looked at Tom, but he was holding his friend's hand.

'See you later.' she said to Tom and allowed the corporal to lead her away. He escorted her between two of the maquees, moving away from the battlefield, until they reached a tent, part-covered in wet mud. There was a small wooden desk inside with three soldiers sitting around it. By the look of their uniforms, they were officers.

'Thank you, Corporal.' said the officer on the far left. They all looked at Vanessa. 'I am acting Captain Klute. Who are you and how did you get here?'

'My name is Vanessa. I came to see Ms Nightingale' she improvised, 'to see if I could be of assistance.'

'Are you a nurse?'

'No, but I thought I could probably help out in other ways.'

The officer stood up 'Nightingale is dead.' he said. She died Tuesday. Shame, she was special. Bloody war!'

'Yes', said Vanessa 'Look, I have had a shock, and forgotten where I am, and a lot of what is going on. Who are we fighting and what's this war about?'

The Captain had an incredulous look 'You don't know who we're fighting?'

'I told you. I was wounded by canon–fire.' She pointed to her head. 'I seem to have lost my memory.'

'That doesn't look serious.' said one of the officers. 'What do you remember?'

'Not much.' said Vanessa. I just found myself here and I don't know who is fighting or why? Everybody looks the same to me'.

'The same!' exclaimed the Captain. 'Come look here.' He led Vanessa out of the tent flap and around to the back. Lying dead, just a few metres away, was a soldier who looked very like Joey whom Tom was sitting with in the hospital tent.

'Look at him!' said the Captain. 'Damned filth. Bloody *lightjack*! Damn them all to hell! How can you say that scum looks the same?'

Vanessa was lost for words. He was wearing white pantaloons, a red jacket and black boots. He was indistinguishable from Joey in the marquee, apart from he had a small scar on his cheek. 'Well? said the Captain. What do you say now? Memory or no memory, you see what we have here?'

'Well, I see he has a little scar!' said Vanessa.

'Screw that! He's a *lightjack,* and you are obviously shell-shocked. Corporal, take this woman to the tents and see if someone can look at her head or something. Then maybe she can help out. We are starting again in ten minutes.'

On the way back to find Tom, Vanessa quizzed the Corporal who was a plain speaking and forthcoming man. By asking some direct questions she was able to find out what the war was about, although she found it almost beyond belief. This terrible war that had been going on for countless generations was over the shades of the red uniform jackets. This side, the *darkjacks*, had an unshakeable hatred of those wearing a very slightly lighter shade of red jacket. All the jackets were crimson. In poor light, and with all the smoke, Vanessa found it incredible that anybody was able to discern the subtle change in shade. And this horrible war had been going on for all those centuries because of that! It was incredible. They all had red blood, and it was being spilled every hour over essentially the same coloured jackets because of a tiny variation in the frequency of light-waves! How could they be so utterly stupid? What a sick thing to spill blood over! A memory stirred in her mind: *There is nothing imaginable, that is so terrible, that human beings do not do it to one another.*

They never reached the hospital tent. A cannonball smashed into the ground right in front of them, and the shrapnel from it tore in all directions. Vanessa was thrown to the ground with the corporal on top of her. His entire body was riddled with metal fragments. She pushed his body off of her, realizing that her head was swimming, and she was too dizzy to stand. A group of six or so soldiers were bearing down on her with their bayonets pointing straight at her. Although she could not tell which shade of jacket they were wearing, she realized that she must have been concussed by the explosion because, shades and tints aside, there was no mistaking that each of these soldiers had the face of a pig! Once again, she prepared for her doom but, once again, fate had another plan for her. The pig-soldiers moved aside for a figure shrouded like a black friar. He looked about seven feet tall and his face was not visible, In fact, it looked like a black hole! It seemed familiar. In fact, Vanessa had the unshakable impression that it was her dark friend from the crypt or, at least, a manifestation of it. She struggled to get to her feet but couldn't move at all. She realized that her body had sunk into the ground as though it were quicksand, but now it was solid and partially encasing her, gripping her, leaving her completely vulnerable. The dark figure did not kneel, but just got nearer like an image getting closer and moving into focus. Now the black hole was filling her vision to the exclusion of all else. Then it exhaled and enveloped her with the breath of death. Incredibly, Vanessa did not feel panic at that moment. Instead, her mind turned to Rio, remembering her when they were very small children, chasing ducks by the river. She could see the sunshine through the leaves of the trees and she remembered Rio's laughter as she fell over, while the ducks scampered away. Then she saw the figure of the dark Friar hovering over Rio and felt its hatred. Rio was in danger! Vanessa lashed out with her mind at the darkness, but it just seized her mind as a man might snatch a wounded fly and she could feel its laughter as it began to squeeze the life out of her and replace it with a venom as cold as the grave.

But now, standing next to Rio by the river, she reached and took her sister's hand, and pushed through the sun gilded leaves with her mind, and reached for the sun itself. She lashed her mind around it. She felt the pulse of the sun and stretched her entire being around it. Then she crushed its mass until she felt its massive energy bursting to escape. She opened her arms and flooded the darkness with the unmitigated and unrepressed force of a quadrillion nuclear explosions and, as she did so, she absorbed some of it, and stored it along the pathways of her mind.

The dark creature recoiled at this incredible onslaught, and Vanessa sensed in the core of her being, its absolute shock at such an unbridled force of energy. Damaged beyond imagination, and stunned beyond belief, it fled leaving the ultra-waves in Vanessa's mind oscillating at millions of times light speeds, and creating a psychic gravitational well that curved thought across time and space. For a moment there, she and Rio had achieved a partial fusion. Just partial, that was a long way short of a full joining of minds. In that limited exchange, Rio had not even been aware of her. She knew that. She had no idea how she knew. And now she felt the ground slipping away from her. Was she losing consciousness, or regaining consciousness? Where was Millie? Vanessa felt connected with everything and everyone, and also with nothing. She felt stretched out thinly, over an unimaginable distance. Then, she felt some hands lifting her. She was looking into the eyes of a copper haired gypsy-woman who lifted a cup to Vanessa's lips. But there was no liquid in it. Vanessa was fighting for breath, but the gypsy pushed the cup towards Vanessa's mouth and, this time, Vanessa drank thirstily from the cup. After several swallows she felt her strength and her balance returning. She was no longer thirsty yet she knew that her lips had not touched water.

Vanessa said 'What was it? In that cup?'

Rhea smiled at Vanessa. 'It was light.' she answered. Then Vanessa felt something touching her leg. It was Tom's drum, and he was smiling at Vanessa. Rhea took the drum from Tom and put it down. Then she took Tom's hand, and Vanessa's hand, and led them away. As they were walking Tom said 'What about Joey? What about my friend?'

Rhea replied 'Don't worry. He's fine now. He has been sent home and you will see him soon. The war is over.'

Tom looked relieved. He said 'Who won?'

Rhea replied, 'The only victor in war, is peace.'

Tom let go of Rhea's hand, and darted between Rhea and Vanessa so that he could walk between them, holding their hands. 'I have a cuckoo.' He said.

Vanessa smiled and said. 'That's nice Tom.'

Chapter 16

Dream-world. Transylvania/Jamaica.

WHEN MILLIE ARRIVED back at the Great Hall, the Count was standing next to the dining table. 'And so?' said the Count.

Yusi said 'She did it. She prevailed.'

'I know that', said the Count. 'Where is she?'

Millie said 'She's gone. When we opened the door, the crypt was empty. Do you not know where she went?'

The Count sat down slowly on a chair and stoked his chin. He said, 'No. I don't know.'

But she's alright? asked Millie. 'She's not hurt?'

The Count said 'Well, yes, she has been hurt. But she has also been strengthened.'

'But she is still herself, I mean?' said Millie, thinking that this was like trying to draw blood out of a stone.

'This is not an exact science', said the Count. 'I can tell you that she was successful. We knew that any success would come at a cost. She has been traumatized by her experience, but she has gained the strength that was intended.'

'Intended by whom?' said Millie

'That would be too much information for this moment.'

But Millie was becoming increasingly impatient. 'No, if you know something, tell me now', said Millie.

The Count did not look ruffled. He did not look like the kind of person that anything could ruffle. 'I have told you that it would not be good to share that information with you at this time. Think of this: If a six-year-old child were to ask you to teach him to drive, would you do it? If he were to insist that you explain the method and then hand over the keys to the car, would you do it?'

'That's different.' said Millie.

'Is it? How do you know? You are, what? Sixteen?'

'Seventeen.'

'Seventeen. Old enough to know that the choices we make are not always the choices that we want to make, but rather the choices that we *need* to make. Look around you. This is a serious place. We are not playing games. Vanessa has moved on with her journey and it is nearly time for you to do the same, unless you want to spend the rest of your life here?'

'No, thank you.' said Millie.

The Count's tone softened. 'It's time for you to get some rest.' The Count looked at his sons. 'One of you, show her the way, she has probably forgotten. Now goodnight, Millie. I will not see you tomorrow, so I want to say how pleasant it was to finally meet you. I am much older than I look so take the advice of a very old man: Try to be patient. Work at it. And remember, even when family members are separated, they are still a family. Distances make no difference. In reality, there is no distance between anything, or anyone. We all exist in the same space and moment. Again, goodnight.' This time there was no half smile; it was a genuine full smile that lit up his face.

It felt strange entering her room without Vanessa being there. As she heard Yusi's footsteps moving away, she just lay down on the bed. This was the pattern of her life it seemed. Everyone she knew was taken away; her mother and her father, Freddy, Donna. Even Geoff whom she had really only met fleetingly but had bonded with during that dream with Tarot and Muna, the tiger. And now Vanessa was gone too. She thought about Muna for a moment, in the palace of the Grand Vizier. Not for a second had she been intimidated by that huge tiger. There had been no sense of danger. She thought about each of them in turn.

Then something hit her like an express train. She was stunned that she had missed it. Freddy had gone looking for *Mark Moore*. Vanessa had spoken about Mark. She was sure Vanessa had said Mark Moore. Millie was not so much remembering what Vanessa had said as what Vanessa had *thought*. Before the Castle, Millie had shared thought streams with Vanessa. Could this be right, or was it too much of a coincidence? Was the man that Freddy had gone looking for, the very same as the one that Vanessa had left in a hotel room as she was dragged out of the hotel room by rogue cops?

Her head was spinning. She closed her eyes. What a day! Or night! Or whatever it was!

There was a faint and distant sound of music coming from somewhere. She focussed on it trying to make out what it was. She could almost make it out. It was reggae. Now she recognized it.

"Don't worry about a'ting. Every little 'ting, gonna be alright".

'CAN I GET YOU SOME-ting?' A Jamaican man with dreadlocks with a wide smile had approached her table. *'How about a 'freshing fruit punch?'* Without waiting for a reply he handed her a large cold glass with decorative fruits around the rim. A couple of umbrellas made it rather difficult to reach the drink. It was lovely.

'First time in Mo'Bay?' he said.

'Mo'bay?'

'Montego Bay. Home of chill.'

Millie looked around. Her table was perched outside a small restaurant on a narrow road, painted mostly pale blue, with occasional splashes of yellow. The early morning sun caused a blinding glint off the few passing cars.

'Yes', said Millie 'This is my first time here.'

'Well this where people come to relax, so you do that' and he smiled again and walked back inside. A Jamaican couple were sitting across

from each other on the next table along, holding hands. They looked so happy, like they didn't have a care in the world. Millie had been thirsty. She had already finished her drink. Her waiter reappeared with another one in his hand for her. Then she remembered that she didn't have any money. She owned up to it.

'*No worries,*' he said, '*pay me next time.*'

'Its nice here.' Millie said.

'*Oh me luv Jamaica Mun*' said the guy with playful smile '*Dem girl dem pretty*' and he winked at Millie. Then he said, '*Look like you doin' lotta tinkin.*'

Millie said, 'I have a lot to think *about.*'

'*Yeah? What a small ting like you gotta tink about?*'

'Well lots of things. I have a lot of planning to do. I am trying to get back to where I came from and to meet up with – with people I got separated from. It seems like I just get moved from place to place without any say in it. Everything I do seems to have unforeseen consequences. So I am trying to take a moment to think things through; to try to come up with a strategy having thought through the potential consequences in advance.

'*That is good tinking. We have a saying for that in Patwa: "Before he buy di trowser, monkey must tink wat to do wit di tail!"* '

Millie laughed 'That's a good one.' she said. Then Millie got the shock of her life. A crocodile climbed up the two steps from the road, and headed towards her table. It was huge.

'*Don't worry your head about him. He come for marshmallows. He your regular vegetarian, don't like meat too much.*' He produced some white marshmallows from his pocket and flicked one at a time at the crocodile whose jaw moved so quickly to catch it, that the motion was a blur. '*But I tell you, it a bad ting not to have dem sweet tings for him.*'

The crocodile continued to stare at the man for a moment, then, as though he had shrugged his shoulders, he turned and headed back on to the road and continued his foraging expedition.

'Does here come here often? asked Millie.

'*Every day. He alright. In Mo'Bay we all brothers and sisters together. Don't want no grief. If there a problem we chew it together and the problem gone. You got something' weighin' you down, maybe you share it wi me an' maybe I can help you. Two heads, you know!*'

'Well, that's kind of you' said Millie, but it's complicated.

'*Now when you say it complicated, what you mean exactly? That it too complicated for a simple mind like mine or that, really, you too lazy to unpack it all on account that it weigh too much?*

'I don't mean either', said Millie. I mean it's so complicated that I do not understand it myself. I am not sure anybody understands it. It is like the whole world has come under attack, from every angle, and everything you thought was one thing turns out to be really something else. And every time you try to retrace your steps and find your way back, seems like you just get pushed further away.'

'*Well in that case, sound like you got a problem so big that you need somethin' real special. More ways than one to crack a coconut. Sound like you need talk wi' Aunty.*'

Aunty? Aunty who?

Just at that moment a young Jamaican girl in a short skirt walked by the front and called out. What she said was incomprehensible to Millie, but there was no doubt that it was friendly ragging. The man shouted something back as she passed out of view then again she could not understand except the final word, '*Babylon.*'

'*She a bad gel.*' he said in a manner that betrayed that he did not consider her entirely without redeeming features.

'I see. You mentioned *Aunty*? said Millie.

The young man had a look in his eyes that suggested his mind was lingering on the young woman who had just headed around the corner.

'*Yeahmun. Di white gel. We call her di white gel.*'

'Because she's white?' Millie suggested with a grin.

'No, because she always wear *white. White skirt, white frilly blouse, white shoe, white hat. Everytin white. I mean she is white, but dat not de reason for di name. Plenty gels round here is white. But she not easy to talk to. She know* everytin. *She not easy to see. Nobody know where she live and nobody been able to speak to her for a long time. She very busy travellin' aroun'. Sometimes she just walk on the beach. Never know when. I pretty sure she will speak to you though.'*

'Really. Why me? What makes you think she would make an exception for me, if she doesn't speak to people as a rule?

'Because you the only new blood aroun' here for a long time. Nobody come here anymore. Used to be a lot visitor here but they closed the port. Ol' Mo, at the big house, say nobody can get through like they used to on account of embargo. So the white gel sittin' on all that know-how all to hersel', 'ceptin maybe she spill for you'.

Millie said 'I'm not sure about that. When you say she knows *everything*, you mean she's very knowledgeable, right?'

No, I means she know EVERYTIN'. Everytin' there is to know, she know. Notin' she don't know. Been here from the beginning.'

'I'm not with you. Been here since the beginning of what?

'What you say your name was?'

'Millie'

'Nice to meet you Millie. My name's Charlie.'

'Yeah, good to meet you Charlie' and she shook his hand formally.

'Can I get you another of those?'

'No, thanks.' He looked disappointed. 'On second thoughts, why not? Yes please. It's lovely.'

Charlie headed slowly back into the restaurant, and she had in mind the advice from the Count: *Be patient*. She looked around, taking in the scenery. Everything looked Caribbean retro. Old, slightly rusted, and distinctly faded signs, that looked like they had been new in the 1940s, were on display here for products like Pear's soap, and Ovaltene. Even the cars that passed occasionally, resembled the types she had only seen in movies of the 1950s. There was something comforting about the place, yet something eerie about it at the same time. She nearly jumped out of her skin when the crocodile returned. Evidently he had been on his return journey and decided to test whether there were, in reality, no more marshmallows to be had. The young couple who had been all starry eyed, on the adjacent table, had moved on. Millie was alone. The crocodile mounted the steps and swung towards her, fixing her directly with his an expression that, for all the world, seemed to have morphed from somewhat disappointed, to outright peeved. Millie decided against screaming, in case it alarmed him into action, but opted for calling for help in a sort of retrained shout.

'Charlie! Charlie! The crocodile has come back!'

Charlie emerged with another drink and stunned Millie by his direct approach. He said to the crocodile *'Hey! C'mon, you had already.'* And he pointed with his finger to where he wanted the crocodile to go - back down the steps. However, the crocodile moved forward towards, Millie and she considered jumping up and running.

'Don't run', said Charlie. *'Stay still.'* Then he tossed one of the little umbrellas from the drink at the crocodile. He batted it away with his head, not distracted and unimpressed. He remained still for a while, as if pondering his options. Then he swung around, descended the stairs, slowly crossed the road, and seemed to be examining an advert for Gale's Honey. Millie felt rather sorry for him. He was out of his element. Obviously, he was hungry, and so long as he was wandering along the streets, he was in danger of being run over. He was also a danger to traffic. Come to think of it, he was a danger to everyone, and yet in this easy going, relaxed and let live community, he was apparently allowed to just mosey around.

Charlie sat down opposite Millie and, after her heart had settled down and she had got back her breath, she sipped the drink. It was different this time. It had a creamy coconut flavour, with the faintest hint of rum with an after-taste of sharp citrus that hit the palette after a surprising delay.

Charlie smiled when he saw her reaction. *'We call it* "The Highwayman" *he said,* '*on account of he take you by surprise.*'

'Oh, that's magic' said Millie having graduated from sipping, to gulping it down. 'Um, you were saying about Aunty? You were saying that she knows everything...'

'She does, mun.'

'And that she has been here since the beginning. The beginning of what? Montego Bay? What? An independent Jamaica?'

Charlie chuckled. *'No Mun. The front end beginning. The beginning of time. The beginning of everytin.' Aunty, here befo' anytin' else. She can do anytin.' She really de real 'deal! Whatever problem you have mun, she can set you straight. She design all this you see here. She, the architect.*'

Chapter 17

Dream-world. Irish Village

THE SHAMROCK PUBLIC House was about twelve miles from Dublin, in a small village. The village bordered the ghost of an airfield that had once hosted hurricane and spitfire pilots, in training, during World War II.

The saloon bar was decked out in Tudor beams with a few, dull, long brass horns, hooked to the wall which had obviously seen better days. It was speckled by an asymmetrical assortment of tables, around which a few men lounged around, on wooden seats with faded covers. In one smoky corner, three men were standing, playing darts. An archaic music system, that struggled even to sound wheezy, piped out Irish rebel songs, and Roy was tapping is his feet to *Johnson's Motor Car* when his opponent took his bishop in one deft movement, and looked suitably triumphant. 'Check,' he said.

'Ah, Jesus,' cursed Roy, and began to move his Knight, until he saw the glint in Michael's eye across the chessboard. Then, for the first time during the game, Roy began to apply a bit of concentration. Rosie McCann, the barmaid, came over, and if ever the term 'buxom' was appropriate, there was no denying that Rosie was top of the list; or "fair, fat and forty", as she had been describing herself for some few years now. As she whisked away the empties, and put a couple of jugs on the now vacated beer mats, she said, 'Michael O'Shea, how many times do you have to be beaten by this man, who is in league with the Devil himself, or his very own son? You know he never loses at anything!' Roy looked at Rosie. It was true. In some ways he was the luckiest man alive.

It seemed that anything at all that he turned his hand to, whether it be chess or cards, or anything that involved even a modicum of luck, he won hands down every single time. Nobody in either village pub would take him on at 'spoofing', a game that involved guessing what amount of coins the other players were holding in their closed fists. It was as if he could see clear through fingers. But he knew he could not. He just invariably knew what they were holding, without any idea how he knew. He smiled, and with a fluid, even graceful movement, swished diagonally across the board with his Queen.

'Mate in two, I think you will find Michael, me boy,' Roy said, and gave Rosie one of those, *well, what can you do?* smiles, as she continued to gaze at the board.

Michael sighed and gently flicked over his King in surrender with the tip of his finger.

'I am the *only* one here who will still give you a game, you jammy flash git, you just remember that!' Michael said, as he got to his feet and announced that he was heading home while glancing, somewhat regretfully, at the half-glass of beer that he was leaving behind on the table. He reached back down to the table and said 'Ah to hell with it', as he downed the remainder in one swig. Then he punched Roy's arm lightly as he passed and added 'Tar-ra you rascal, and goodnight to you Rosie' and headed in an unsteady zig-zag to the door and attempted to open it. But the door remained shut, and the handle came off in his hand.

'Would you bloody believe it?' he exclaimed, looking back at Rosie, who was laughing with one hand on her hip. It could not be said that Michael O'Shea shared in any measure of the luck that surrounded Roy. But Michael was not loved any less for being clumsy and ungainly and prone to bad luck. On the contrary, he was loved the more for it. Barely a second later, came the bell for last orders.

'One more for the road?' Rosie asked Roy, in a tone that subtly implied that it would be one too many.

'No, I think I'll call it a night. I'm counting on you seeing me safely home, Rosie, if I wait 'till you've closed up.'

The walk home from *The Shamrock* was less than ten minutes. Roy looked up at the stars, and enjoyed the summer breeze with his arm around Rosie's waist. The front door to his cottage was unlocked, as usual. Roy poured himself a whisky while Rosie headed straight upstairs. A little while later, she walked down again with her hair wet from the bathroom. She wiggled on to his lap, and into his arms.

The water from her hair was dripping on to Roy's arms. Roy wiped it evenly across his skin.

Rosie said, 'Are you never going to make an honest woman of me, Roy Docherty? Am I to skulk around like a shameless hussy for the rest of me days?' He didn't answer. He leaned forward and kissed her on the tip of her nose. Then he took a firm grip of her pulled her body into him. She gasped.

'You like being a shameless hussy.' He said 'But if I marry anyone Rosie, I swear it will be you. You are the only person I've ever really cared about.' Then his expression really clouded, and for a moment he looked rather sad.

'What is it?' Rosie asked.

'It's nothing'

'Tell me'

'No, really Rosie, it's all in the past.'

'Tell me Roy, I want to hear it. I want us to share everything. No secrets. What! Do you think I'm a good time girl, who ups and runs, at the first hint of the laughter dying down?'

Roy stared at the flames in the log fire. Then he turned his head back to Rosie and said, 'I don't know what's happening to me these days, Rosie. Something has changed, and I can't put my finger on it. We all have a past. Well, recently, it has felt like I have more than one past! I know that sounds daft, and no, I'm not drunk – on my way, perhaps – but not there yet. I had a dream the other day in which I had a wife and daughter, in America. I tried to put it out of my mind, but it keeps coming back. It's like, water seeping onto a small boat while you're struggling to keep it out. But you can't!'

Rosie said 'I think you are just over-tired. You don't sleep enough! You are up most of the night doing god know what! And you have always had one hell of an imagination. And all that beer and whisky can't be a big help. Alcohol amplifies dreams and imaginings.'

'That's just it.' said Roy. 'I don't think these are dreams and imaginings. I think they are, like, you know, repressed memories.'

'And just why would you be having repressed memories?' Rosie asked, getting up from his lap and sitting down on the sofa next to him. 'More likely it was a vivid dream. Sometimes with those, they can seem so real that you have a clear waking memory of the dream; just the same as if it were a genuine memory.'

Roy said 'It was too detailed to be a dream. It felt too real.'

'Well, of course, it felt real. Dreams do feel real. That's the point of them. Go on then, what were these details? Describe it to me. Maybe I can help you to come to terms with it, if it's bothering you so much.'

Roy looked reluctant to go into, it but Rosie put her hands on either side of his face, looked him in the eyes, and said 'Roy?'

Roy reached for his whisky, but the glass was empty. That was another thing. That did not usually happen. If he reached for a drink, normally, there would be one there. His magical luck seemed to be running out.

'I'm listening.' prompted Rosie.

'Well, it was like this. I was living in New York, in one of those apartments like you see on the TV. I had a wife.'

'A wife! What was her name?'

'I don't know. I can't remember. But she died, I remember that. It was very sudden. And I had a small daughter, who looked like her mother, except....'

'Yes?'

'Well, she had these amazing eyes that shone with an unnatural light. People used to say that her eyes were *diamonds*.'

'That's nice. So what happened next, in the dream?'

'I could see how upset Millie was by her mother's passing.'

'Your daughter was called Millie?'

'Yes, she was named after my aunt.'

Rosie said 'Alright, so then what?'

'Well, I wanted to make it better for Millie but I couldn't. I just couldn't. That's where the dream stopped. And it has left me with this, sort of ache; a terrible emptiness. It hurts. I'm sorry, maybe it is just too much whisky.'

Rosie took both his hands in hers and said 'Dreams can affect us Roy. There are a lot of things about them that we do not understand. We carry our dreams with us all the time, and we dream all the time we are awake – in the background where we hardly notice. Without our dreams, we could not exist. They are that important. We can lose our legs, or our arms, or even a lung; and survive. We can replace our hearts and even repair our brains. But without our ability to dream, we would not even register as plant life. Even plants dream – yes, they do!'

Roy said 'Are you sure that you have not been drinking, Rosie?'

'I have not had a drop.' said Rosie. 'Let me ask you something, and I want a straight yes or no answer: do you think that you have a daughter, somewhere, called Millie?'

'I don't know. Honestly, I don't.'

'Well let me reframe the question: Do you *feel* that you have a daughter?'

'Yes. I do feel that. Yes, I do.'

Rosie said 'Well then our path is clear. We search under every rock and stone until we find her. We get to the bottom of this, once and for all. We *have* to know.'

Chapter 18

The Moon and Mythology

'GOOD MORNING DAVID.' said Geoff, as he and Donna seated themselves at the breakfast table. 'You don't look happy.'

'I'm not happy, no.' said David. 'I am afraid I have not good news for you. There are no transports running at the moment. There is a moon-wide lockdown because of the troubles. I am afraid we are stranded here for a while. It is a very bad business.'

'For how long?' asked Donna. 'And what's the latest news?'

David put his coffee down. 'The rioting has spread everywhere. It is happening on Earth too, although they are better equipped and resourced to manage crowd control there. Here, there are just not enough security teams. And the fact that policing here is almost entirely handled by robots, droids and synths, is making things worse. They tend to react by rote, without any of the finessing and discretion applied in traditional policing. Right now, rigid approaches to population control are back-firing. When people are hurt by other people there are angry responses, but when people are injured by machines, well, the reaction is a lot worse. Resentments have grown exponentially in just a few hours, and all public transportation has been temporarily suspended. That is, suspended until law and order is restored. Right now, the situation is getting worse, not better. You see,' he looked at Donna 'the latest reports about the new planet have increased the panic on Earth, and here.'

He nodded towards the Earth, that was visible through the window. 'But it is even worse here, because of the sense of isolation and exposure people feel out here. There are a lot of misunderstandings about living on the moon. The first is that people generally do not realize how precarious ordinary life is here. For example, the extremes of temperature between 130 degrees when it's light and minus 130 degrees when it is dark, makes for potentially dangerous changes on the lunar surface. Seismic shifts and eruptions, for example, pose a threat to all oxygenated environments. And then there are the meteor strikes, because of a lack of atmosphere. They are mostly very small, but very high velocity projectiles from space can penetrate all but our strongest defences in seconds. They mostly impact the far side where we have only unmanned deep space telescopes and listeners, but near side impacts are also a constant threat. They do happen here. There was a new crater created just five weeks ago not so very far from here. There was nothing to damage there, fortunately. But it could have hit this very hotel and anyway if the impact had been just a little bit nearer, yes, yes, it could have shaken the foundations. And now the latest news about this rogue planet has found a very receptive audience in our increasingly paranoid lunar population.'

Geoff was becoming impatient. David was obviously not getting to the main event. 'Cut to the chase, David. What is the latest news about the new planet?' said Geoff.

David looked at both Geoff and Donna in turn. He said, 'The news is not very heartening. Although we still have no exact readings about the planet's mass and exact velocity, we have been able to make a reasonably accurate projection, based on mapping its progress against the stars using telescopes. It has taken everybody by surprise. Even allowing for significant margins for error, that planet like body is moving inwards at an unbelievable speed, and will either impact the Earth or pass so close that the tidal effect will knock us out of the sun's orbit.' He paused. 'Really, we have never know anything to move as fast as this planet thing. It is very much faster than the fastest comet recorded.' He took in a deep breath and avoided their eyes. 'We have maybe four days. Not more.'

Nobody spoke for a moment. Then Donna said 'I just want to be clear about this. What you are saying is that we have no possible way of stopping that planet thing and that, one way or another, directly or indirectly, it is going to impact us. So, we have four more days to live. The only human beings left alive anywhere, will be those working on the Mars colony.'

Geoff said gently 'The workers on Mars are synthetics and androids. There are no humans there now. They left after the novelty of being there had worn off. There is no breathable atmosphere on Mars and it is not a convenient journey like it is between the Earth and Moon. So, excepting a miracle, it looks like all human life we will all be gone.'

Donna said 'I don't believe that. I absolutely do not believe that. No. I don't know what's going on here but I feel certain that we are not just going to be swept away. There is a reason why we are here. We haven't come this far just to be wiped out.'

Geoff said, 'The Architects again?'

Donna said 'If you had felt what I felt Geoff, those incredible minds, you would be as certain as I am that this story is not over. We need to press on and find Millie. I don't care what anybody say or thinks. I know she has something to do with this. This is all connected. I know it is.'

Geoff said 'Your devotion to Millie is astounding as it is remarkable Donna, but with only four days to go, rescuing her is not really the same priority as it was.'

Donna said 'But it *is* Geoff. There is a direct link with the planet, I absolutely know that, although I cannot explain how. There is a much bigger picture here that we are not seeing; that we are not being *allowed* to see.'

David interrupted, having seen something on one of the wall screens. He pointed, and Geoff and Donna looked behind them.

'Oh, come on!' said Donna 'I don't believe it.'

Standing side by side, as if they were standing together, was a huge picture of Donna and the Mona Lisa.

David looked at a loss. Geoff said 'Some tourists took a picture of Donna next to the Mona Lisa in the National Gallery in London. Someone must have played with the photo and uploaded it. You wouldn't think people would be interested in a photo at a time like this!'

But the caption running along the bottom simply read: *Can it be true?*

Donna said 'What? Can what be true?'

David said 'It's all just paranoid speculation. You shouldn't be worried with it?'

Donna said 'Please, just answer the question. What are they talking about?'

David looked uncomfortable. 'It's absurd. Do you remember the story of Perseus and Andromeda?'

Donna replied 'Not off hand, no.'

Geoff charged in 'Oh, come off it, David. Nobody could be that ignorant and stupid!'

Donna said 'Will somebody *please* tell me what is going on?'

Geoff said 'It's a convoluted story in Greek mythology. But the relevant bit is, obviously, that the King Cephus's daughter, Andromeda, is chained to a rock by the sea as a human sacrifice in place of the whole city being destroyed by, Cetus, the sea monster unleashed by Poseidon. Perseus rescues Andromeda, in the story, and kills the monster.'

Donna just sat quietly in thought.

David said 'Don't worry. These people are crazy. They are spreading this absolute nonsense that the planet will destroy us all unless.... I mean, it is just absolute nonsense!'

Donna said 'So what do they want to do? Chain me to a cliff? And then what? The planet reaches out its hands and takes me, but doesn't touch the rest of anything? I mean, where does this idea come from?'

David said 'I told you the whole idea was crazy. Apparently the idea comes from dreams. A lot of people have claimed to have had dreams in which they have been informed that your sacrifice would save all the people. Even you!'

Geoff said 'That is quite enough of this absolute nonsense!'

But Donna said 'No. I want to hear this. How are they saying that I would also survive then?'

Geoff shook his head with irritation but Donna held David's gaze.

David said 'Geoff is right that this isn't worth getting into, it is all too far- fetched and irrelevant.'

'It is not irrelevant to me!' said Donna.

David sighed. 'What these lunatics are saying is that the moon should be evacuated; except for you. Whatever it is that is controlling, or riding in that planet, would "absorb" you. But there is nothing to suggest that it wants you dead. All the indications from those that were interviewed about their dreams, point to the fact that you are wanted alive. But, as I say, the whole thing is madness.'

Now Geoff stood up. 'That is enough about this rubbish. Nobody is evacuating the Moon and this whole hysterical story is the most absurd nonsense that I have ever heard. There is absolutely no chance that Donna would be left alone on the Moon. The prospect of evacuation has not even been discussed.'

A member of staff approached. 'Excuse me,' the synthetic said in a feminine dispassionate voice. 'Would you please gather in the main conference hall. There is going to be an announcement.'

'What kind of announcement?' asked Geoff

'I have not been informed officially. But I understand that they want to begin an evacuation of the Moon. It is being called "Operation Dunkirk."

THE STORY CONCLUDES in "Reality Rebooted", the final part of The Dream Corporation Trilogy.

Book 3: The Dream Corporation
Reality Rebooted

REALITY REBOOTED IS the final part of the Dream Corporation Trilogy. It culminates in bringing all our characters together towards a spectacular and utterly satisfying finale. In this final part of the story, we learn what has *really* been going on, and what we learn leads towards a nail-biting climax. Even more dramatic adventures are to come, but, eventually, all the characters that we have come to know, enjoy touching meetings or reunions. They combine their strengths and talents in ways that surprise and stun everybody. The solutions that are deployed to cope with the complex challenges before them, rely on the science of the mind, and its connection with universal consciousness, gravitational fields, curves in space, dark energy, and anti-matter. Tarot's genius unravels all the big mysteries that have confounded us over millennia including what happens when we die?; and is there other intelligent life in the universe?

And the big secret is that, fiction aside; Tarot really does give us the answers! The knowledge in "Reality Rebooted" will change the world forever; for everybody.

This Trilogy does not merely have a big ending. It has a colossal ending and the blueprint for a new beginning, in a vastly different reality.

Other forthcoming titles from Michael  Williams

The Man Who Lived Backwards

THE POLICE STATION was unusually quiet. Sergeant Reece hastened to see Inspector Nichols in his office. She said, 'Sorry to disturb you, Sir. You will know that the Vice President had a heart attack at about half-past one today. He was eating lunch with the President and the First Lady in the Rose Garden, along with Senators Morley, Prince and Rodriguez.

'Yes. Of course, I know that. As a matter of fact, I have just heard the terrible news that the Vice-President has died in St Catherine's hospital. It's very sad. Why are you here Sergeant?'

'Well, we have a man in custody downstairs, who claims that he lives backwards, and says that our tomorrow, is his yesterday.'

'Right! So he is crank. Why bother me with this?'

'Well Sir, the thing is, he had this piece of paper with him when I arrested him at 10.15 this morning, as he was trying to break into the Hume laboratory facility in Oakland. Take a look at it.'

The Inspector reached for it and stared at it for a few moments. through small black spectacles. His expression underwent several changes until it settled upon complete bewilderment and high agitation.

The Inspector exclaimed, 'My God! He has the whole thing right, in every single detail! The Senators names – everything! And it says right here that you would give me this paper after the VP's death had been announced! This is just not possible!'

Sergeant Reece said 'There's more. He claims that we have to stop a virus being created that will lead to the annihilation of every human being. He says that it will seem to have emerged from China, and the first series of waves are merely a prelude to a mutation that is fatal and unstoppable. He says we have to stop it *today*. Tomorrow he will be gone. He will have passed into yesterday!'

What the Devil!

BRIAN PERCY SAT STARING out of the cafe window, admiring the wide Paris Boulevard, with the trees wearing the ravages of winter. He had a strong black coffee. It was still a bit too early in the year to be sitting outside. Should he change that? After all, he was God. That said, he wasn't accustomed to his new job yet, by any means. Late yesterday, he had attended a job interview for the post of Administrator in the Tenderloin District of San Francisco.

When the recruiters revealed that they had the position of God on offer, given that the previous incumbent had gone fishing in Vancouver – he had thought that they were joking! They had not been. But when he accepted the job, he still considered it to be just part of a test.

He was given a long list of rules that God could break if he wished, but they had cautioned that the consequences would be very dramatic. Brian's first appointment was with the Devil. Now, as arranged, he was waiting at the Devil's favourite little spot, but his adversary was already late arriving.

Brian was distracted by a passing scooter, when a well groomed, clean shaven man, wearing an Armani suit, pulled up a chair.

'I'm Tony de Luca.' he said. 'Congratulations on your new job. I have done this many times, so if you don't mind, I am going to dive right in. But first, I want to clear up a fundamental misunderstanding. Being the Devil is a professional position, just like yours. I am not "evil" nor do I want to make mischief. In fact, I got the job because I am eminently reasonable. If I wanted to do real damage, you would be amazed at how much of it I could do! I get a very bad press, but I am actually a nice guy! Truly, I hate some aspects of my job. Before you ask, you are my fifty-second God, and, as a matter of fact, that lack of continuity causes me as many problems as it does everybody else.'

He seemed to lose concentration for a moment. 'Look at the dust on this table! And that is cigar ash, look! That is bad. Standards are dropping here. The new management is sloppy! I hate sloppiness. Now where was I? Right you are, so, you are one in a line of Gods of generally high ability but, to be clear, I have been here from the very beginning. I am the professional here. In fact, you could say that nobody has more experience in their job than I do. Obviously, my responsibility is to oppose you, but too much disruption helps nobody, so I hope we can co-operate, as far as the rules allow. Now obviously, you are omnipotent, but not omniscient yet. It takes a long time to "download" all knowledge into any one mind. You could say that that is where I get an initial advantage.'

He looked at his Rolex. 'Now look, sorry this was short, but I have to go. The Devil's work is never done! We can meet again, once you've had a chance to get moved in. Oh, by the way, I am obliged to tell you this at our first meeting. I don't like the label "Prince of Lies" but the fact is, you cannot rely on everything that I tell you. Dissembling is in my job description, and I really have very little flexibility in that regard. In fact, given that we have different objectives, things can get a bit testy at times, so I hope we will be able maintain mutual respect. Now, all that being said, did they mention the Fundamental Design to you?'

Brian shook his head and Tony de Luca continued 'No? Oh, they are getting careless! Well, just quickly then; don't meddle with the past, or the weather, until you really know what you're doing. Affairs of the heart though, are child's play. You can have a lot of fun with that. I like your hair, by the way. You are one of the handsome ones. Very nice! Au revoir!'

Synopsis

Brian soon learns that being God is, by far, the most difficult job in the world; well, everywhere really!

And being all powerful, without being all knowing, is, in fact, a terrible combination. He has so many questions, but nobody except the

Devil to ask. And the Devil's answers cannot be trusted. Critically, he wants to know how long it will take for the knowledge he needs to do his job properly, to be "downloaded" into his mind. He cannot find out. He has no staff. He cannot get a straight answer about that. He had expected Gabriel and Michael to be on hand, backed up by a heavenly host. But there was no sign of them and the Devil told him, with a petulant wave of his hand, that he was not at liberty to discuss such matters.

And it turns out that the Fundamental Design is complicated, but the second part of the Charter, "The Fundamental Principles", are even more difficult to get to grips with. This is because he cannot even discover what the Fundamental Principles are! The Devil proves increasingly evasive. The one thing that does make a sort of grudging sense is that God is not technically allowed simply to make the world perfect; like with a wave of the wand. To so do would create an *Eden*, an environment totally unfit for homo- sapiens but, moreover, would involve the complete removal of free will. Humans might wish to create robots, but that was definitely not the idea for mankind.

Withal, Brian feels very alone, and his thoughts turn to his first love, Andrea, from his university days. They had become quite close in their final year, but then, Andrea had met a mountain climber and built a life with him. Only that life had turned out to have been an unhappy one. Brian had not been privy to the details, but apparently the drinking and womanizing had become too much for her, and that, together with not having children, which he knew she craved, had led her to take her own life. She had jumped from a bridge. If ever there was a temptation to use his position for the greater good, this was it. The charming Tony de Luca had warmly assured him that he could nip back in time to his university days, woo Andrea, and change the narrative. The Devil had said that he could personally guarantee that this small change would have no effect, at all, on the path of history. And, in all fairness, the Devil had said that God would have to leave Andrea to make the decision about her future, herself. No messing with her mind. Free will was sacrosanct.

Should he do it? Was it that simple? Really, it boiled to down to one thing: Could the Prince of Lies be trusted in this, or was this a trap? I mean, it was not like he was thinking about changing the outcome of a war or anything momentous like that! History would go on as before, wouldn't it? Didn't Andrea deserve another chance?

Biography of the small Bodyguard

THIS SMALL ASIAN LADY, who was battered as a child, toughened up. She could kick a cigarette from behind a heavyweight boxer's ear before he could raise his arms. As a professional, she had protected the Sultan of Brunei, as well as Pavarotti, BB King. President Clinton, and President Nelson Mandela. She was hired by the US Department of Defense to train special forces in unarmed combat, once they thought that they had nothing left to learn. They soon learnt otherwise.

It was her instinct for impending danger, and her forensic attention to detail, that gave her an special edge. She was turned down for a job protecting the Pope, and he was shot the very next day. I know, you have never heard about her. Well, that was the nature of her business. But after she had retired, she told me her story in her home. She made me laugh out loud, and she absolutely dazzled me. We drank tea all afternoon and she had so many stories that it was a good job that I had a recording device on my phone.

As she showed me out, I noticed a black and white picture of her sparring with Bruce Lee. There had been so much to tell, she hadn't mentioned it. But what she did say then about the relationship between Bruce Lee and Jackie Chan, when they all worked together on "Enter the Dragon", could fill a book on its own.

This story will lift your spirits and leave you with a deeper understanding of human nature.

EXTRACT FROM BIOGRAPHY of the small Bodyguard
When An Lin spoke, there was a charming vulnerability in her voice that juxtaposed with the high adrenalin sequences that she was

describing. This is an accurate transcription from An Lin's account, with her own vocal inflexion and accent, as faithfully as I was able to reproduce from the original voice recording:

'I was nervous because I am basically shy. But anyway, I did not have to speak. The soldiers were lined up in two line in front of me, behind the gym mat, and the officer next to me introduced. He was Captain.

This is An Lin. An Lin and I work as a team to add polish right at the end of training programmes such as the one you have near-completed. There are no fighting men who are better than you, anywhere in the world, apart from the ones that An Lee has polished. Quite a lot of the men grin. One or two gave "eye".

They look at me, and I see they don't believe. They see me as small girl, and because their training very long, and hard, they don't believe I can teach them anything. That is alway' the same problem that people in my business have: too much confidence. So Captain continue *We will work this for three days. That is it. Anybody here who thinks that he is trained enough already, can be excused.* Nobody move. But Captain see one of them near middle and say to him *Sergeant Pope, you were top of the three-niners, correct?* He say yes, so Captain tell him to face me on mat.

Then he say *Take a hold of her. Secure her.* There are four mat in a square, with plenty room. He try to grab me, but although he move fast, he too slow. He cannot touch me. Also, I do not touch him. I move around him for maybe one minute and he still cannot touch me. Now the men are laughing and Captain say *Alright stop. This could go on forever. We know she is faster than you. An Lin, stand where you are. Now Sergeant, take her.* Already I know what he will do. I see his movement before he make it. Just the way his body look, give him away. He reach for me bringing up his right hand, but I use ju-jitsu block and, while he just a little bit off balance, I hook his ankle very hard with my foot and punch the upper middle of his chest with the lower palm of my hand. I do not want to hurt him. Just make him fall backwards into his most vulnerable position. Believe me, this happen very, very quickly. Speed; the only thing that improves technique is lightning speed. This time, the men no laughing. You think, and then you move, is wrong. You think and move same time, is right. That is enough to make the difference between the very good, and the best. In my business, half a second, a very long time.

So, anyway, we train together three day, and I really like it. I like America a lot. I learn from them too. They teach me to sing army song and swear like trooper! But one more thing also I learn in America; you can be hard man, but also have soft heart. Then, on third day, one man come to watch. I do not know he Secret Service until later, when I meet President Clint-On and First lady. That not in the "White Hou". It during campaign in Alabama. I like Alabama. But someone trying to kill him. My job, make sure he cannot do!'

Tales From Two Square Metres

THIS IS A COLLECTION of twelve short stories, each having a very different character and flavour. The stories are set in Mauritius, Jamaica, Brazil, Costa Rica, Cuba, Panama, The Dominican Republic, the Philippines,, Cameroon, Morocco, Lithuania and Transylvania.

These stories are constructed to bring some sunshine to your day, or some warmth to your nights.

Global #1 Bestseller, Star Trek: Captain James T Kirk

MICKY IS A HUGE FAN of Gene Rodenberry's vision for a future for mankind that is multi-cultural, gender neutral, and inclusive. Because of its success and reach, Micky believes that the Star Trek franchise has helped promote better social awareness about ourselves and our planet, and has helped educate us into seeing a world of people, rather than a group of Nations with borders. He is an idealist. He writes a novel called "Award Winning Global #1 Best Seller Star Trek: James T Kirk." He hopes the key-word algorithms will generate a large number of sales. It works. But, unfortunately, he finds himself in Court on charges of deliberately misleading prospective buyers into believing the book is, in fact, an award winning best seller. He is charged with several counts of fraud.

On the day of the trial, his book, which actually was a very good one, has become a best seller and won awards. In fact, William Shatner himself enjoyed it, and endorsed the book. With the publicity of the case, and the landmark trial, the book is, in fact, just days away from becoming the World's Number 1 Bestseller. The prosecution argued cogently that it was Micky's intention to mislead and defraud, and that the self-fulfilling prophesy argument was irrelevant. The law takes fraud very seriously, and is not easily swayed by sentiment. Also, we have not realized Gene Roddenberry's vision quite yet. The law still values property above people. There seemed no possible way for Micky to stay out of jail.

Hundreds of Trekkers show up at the Court to show solidarity, but even Micky's imagination was trumped when Captain Kirk took the stand in full Starfleet uniform, as a witness for the defence. His opening words were, "I don't believe in no-win scenarios."

The Happiness Index

THE PURSUIT OF HAPPINESS is in the US Constitution as a fundamental human right and it is a fundamental goal everywhere. Everybody wants to be happy. Some people are only happy when they are being miserable; but then they enjoy a kind of contentment. And then are those who have enjoyed great success and everything seemed to be going almost too well. They begin to worry that it seems too good to last. Everybody is happy up to a point. Is there a limit to how happy we can be, in the way that there is a limit to how much vitamin C we can absorb in one day? Or are we inhibited by some naturally occurring safeguard in the form of a chemical in our brain? Before the phrase "Pride cometh before a fall" entered the vernacular, there were serious misgivings about enjoying life too much. In the early Greek and Roman civilizations, being too successful was equated with hubris: equating one's mortal self with the gods.

There are so many questions. Here's another: Can happiness be defined, and if it can, then what is the definition? The Oxford English dictionary gives it as: "The state of pleasurable contentment: deep pleasure in, or contentment with, one's circumstances." Hmm! That doesn't really help. We know, dictionary definitions are a snapshot of a word; they do not convey the scale and scope of the meaning and, therefore, they can only be accurate up to a point. Being happy is the opposite of being sad, but it is more than that. Happiness is contentment, but it is also more than that.

It is all well and good having the pursuit of happiness as a right, and having happiness as a goal, but if we are not entirely sure what it is, how can we measure it? We are complicated. Sometimes we are happy, when we are also sad.

Different things make different people happy. Does this mean then that happiness is subjective and can only measured by personal tastes, desires and wants? If so, how is it that highly successful, wealthy, and powerful people are in a proportionately high suicide group? And by contrast, many people relate tales about a desperately poor childhood, but remember all the happiness with nostalgia. And do people who meditate daily, and seek spiritual enlightenment, hold the key. Should we simply heed the Dali Lama? Or are we so diverse that this kind of introspective approach does not work for a lot of people.

There are answers to these questions. There is an *index* by which we can measure happiness for ourselves, and once equipped with that knowledge, we can tailor make approaches and solutions that will actually make us happier. It is within our reach to be more content, more relaxed, more fulfilled and better able to spread happiness. It is not mystical hocus-pocus and it does not require any special effort or concentration.

"The Happiness Index" is not trying to sell you a message, or convert to you to any belief or way of life. It is a sociological, psychological, neurological, economic and historical analysis based on facts, not ideologies, taking account of health, evolution, sex, love, money, beliefs, politics, friendship, law, discovery and attainment.

It is a straight-forward look at what happiness truly is, without jargon, and big words designed to impress like "ethno-methodology" and *sine que non*. It strips away the myths, misconceptions and deliberate falsehoods that impact our happiness and actually impede our progress.

Most importantly, it is not an academic work to gather dust on the shelves of the WHO or the OECD. It offers practical guidance for people who have problems in their lives. Money worries, marital troubles, problems at work, depression, lack of self-worth, loneliness, bereavement, acute anxiety and more.

The Happiness Index has no magic. It has the aggregated collective wisdom to help deal with problems and make anyone's life happier. Anyone at all, can move further up the Happiness Index. You have it in you. You just need to know how to unlock it. No matter how hard life gets, you could make it easier. It will cost you nothing to make the necessary changes.

The Happiness Index will soon be available free, perpetually.

Young Nero

LUCIUS DOMITIUS AHENOBARBUS is a bit of a mouthful. No wonder people prefer the name "Nero". Posterity has also saddled him with persecuting Christians, and for blaming them for the fire. This is completely unsubstantiated. Increasingly, historians dispute this. The bad press that he received is now commonly attributed to the fact that he had an enormous residence of stone built over the remains of wooden Rome. He also stipulated that the new city had to be built out of stone, which added to the expense and caused delays. Yes, this was unpopular. But the real reason that he was disliked was much less to do with buildings, than it was about the kind of man he was.

He was theatrical and effeminate by nature, and loathed the sort of cruelty that was regularly put on show in the Roman arenas. He was squeamish. He hated gladiatorial contests and also cruelty to animals and actually had a safari park in his garden where the animals could roam freely, in well compartmentally segregated zones. He had theatres built and sponsored huge athletic Greek style contests that were the prototype for the "Olympic Games". But the Romans loved their blood-sports second only to bread. Nero supplanted these barbaric events with performances of skilled sports and the arts. He staged Greek plays, in particular, that came across as precious, and often dealt with metaphysical matters, such as Aristophanes' "The Clouds". This was incomprehensible to the masses.

He was a man out of step with his time, and he came to be really hated for it. Here was an Emperor who was closing down bloody arena games, and chariot racing and gambling. He had to go. Nothing destroys a reputation quite like being accused of matricide and debauchery and, to stay in character with the time and place, they say that there is no smoke without fire. So, just as the daggers went into Julius Caesar in the Senate, the daggers went into Nero's reputation, and things went down for him very quickly from there. That was especially the case when it came to his personal bodyguard: The Praetorian Guard. Emperors relied upon them completely. They were selected from the most seasoned soldiers in the Empire, including battle hardened veterans derived from German barbarian tribes. The Praetorian guardsmen had no truck with Greek plays and painted faces! Aristophanes? Please!

In the event, the Romans regained their gladiatorial sports on a larger scale than ever, after Nero's death. After "the year of the four Emperors", the Emperor Vespasian, a shrewd man by any standards, and who enjoys an excellent reputation to this day, restored the games, tore down Nero's house and garden, and built the Roman Coliseum over it. Some of Nero's magnificent house remains buried underneath. The Coliseum is a lasting monument to the glory and cruelty that is synonymous with Rome, as well as an astonishing architectural achievement. This book is about Nero and his family; the facts, not the gossip. But that does not mean that there is not plenty of fun. Nero was funny! For example, the accounts of how he tried do to get his mother out of the way, and she kept reappearing to his chagrin, are hilarious. He even sent her away to sea in a ship under heavy guard, but she jumped overboard and swam back! The truth about Nero is actually far more entertaining than the fiction. He should be remembered as the funniest of the Roman Emperors and, in fact, the funniest ruler there ever was or, at least, the quirkiest! It was Nero who invented the sea-life aquarium, with dolphins and orcas. He had one in his front garden!

The Miner

THE TALE IS SET IN a traditional coal mining village in South Wales. The routine of home and village life, together with the hardship of life at the coal face, is brought vividly to life.

The miner has a secret that he believes would undermine his reputation as a hardy Welshman, if it were discovered. He locks himself away in his cellar at night, and neither his wife nor his children know what he does in there.

Then, one afternoon there is a cave-in at the pit, and the miner is taken to hospital. Thinking that he may pass, he tells his wife and friend his secret before they would discover it for themselves. It turns out that, alone in his cellar, he painted water-colour landscapes of the USA and Canada. He yearned for wide open spaces. Fortunately, he makes a recovery, and it is then that his friend confides that he too has been keeping a secret. But in his case, if the secret were to be revealed, it had the potential to topple the Government in one single day. Coal was not the only thing that was lying buried.

Our Future With the Virus
How will the world change?

NOBODY KNOWS FOR SURE what the future holds. Yet, from our earliest times we have had sooth-sayers, astrologers, tea-leaf and palm readers, clairvoyants and a wide assortment of people in the business of predicting the future. And it always has been a huge business, even in the time of the early Pharaohs, six thousand years ago. So, it is a bit disappointing that we did not have a better warning about Covid-19. We could have done with a road map, alerting us to it. And it would have been helpful to have been able to plan for variants. Even now, if somebody were to step forward with a clear vision of how things will definitively move from here, that person would be a sensation overnight. Countless lives could be saved.

But for people with more scepticism, or those with more of a scientific leaning, it is possible to make certain predictions extrapolated from what we have learned already. This book concentrates on the science, the economics, the cultural dynamic and the politics that the virus has impacted.

We have seen some dramatic changes already, and not all for the bad. And where there have been changes for the bad, some good has come out of it. Some are obvious, and some less so. Air travel has reduced, which is upsetting for those in the aviation sector, but air pollution is down. There has been an increase in domestic violence, but the subject has received much more attention and with growing awareness of a problem comes political will to make improvements in the home but also broader areas of safety. Less obvious things are in play too. There has been a massive reduction in bullfighting. Spain, Portugal, Latin America and even France have seen bull-rings closed. This is bad news for the industry, but good news for bulls and for those who dislike cruelty to animals. And in Spain especially, it is causing a lot of re-assessing of the sport.

Sadly, health services are facing a massive back-log of people needing urgent help for non-Covid conditions. But again, some good news, health workers, and those working alongside them keeping the system going, are starting to be appreciated more highly for the crucial work that they do. Salaries and conditions for them are going to improve, if politicians continue to care about votes.

The virus has had a huge impact on diplomatic relations, and it is pretty obvious that tensions between the haves, and the have-nots, will grow. In the end though, the whole world needs to be healed, not just parts of it. The Earth is like a body; it is connected up. Curing a foot while leaving the rest of the body riddled with disease will not work. Yet, if the divisions between Countries grow, there will be military escalation. Tensions are running much higher than normal. Relations between China, the US and Russia are changing. India and Pakistan relations are coming under increasing pressure, as Covid grows, and resources diminish. These are countries with large conventional forces sitting around, and nuclear arsenals are increasing. The resource issues between North and South Korea is likely to become more problematic. There is a lot of fire power there too. Tensions within China itself are growing, and questions about whether China was truthful to the world about the origins of Covid are simmering, but could come to the boil. And China's obvious plans for Taiwan and Hong Kong are problematic in several ways.

Meanwhile, within countries, tensions are rising. Shortages, lock-downs that restrict freedom of movement, and people just having more time on their hands to think about their gripes, is going to see a rise in protests world-wide. Add to that, the dramatic rise in unemployment world-wide, and the ramifications grow. After all, in the majority of the world, having no employment means no rice to eat. We can expect a lot more people to take to the streets. This will be met with stricter policing and security measures that will generate even more unrest. This will be the case in Europe, Australia and the United States, not just the usual hotspots. This unrest is certain because Covid has disturbed our mental equilibrium. We have been frightened and stressed, and when that happens our bodies generate the chemicals that make us more combat-ready. This is not merely common sense; it is bio-chemistry. That being said, this is the first time in human history that human beings have been united against a common enemy. We have seen a huge increase in scientific co-operation. We know that large numbers of companies that usually compete, are co-operating across many sectors in this "new normal".

And even our stubborn politicians, with their often entrenched positions, are starting to see that the long term solution must have less emphasis on National interests and more attention given to solutions that work for us all, The Earth is an island. Nations cannot afford to remain so, if we are to have any hope of ridding our home of this plague.

For people who can accurately read our future in the stars, this book will be of no help. But for anybody else, this was written with you in mind.

Turned Upside Down

AN INCALCULABLE NUMBER of people have been injured and killed by their own loved ones.

It is a terrible thing to be harmed in your own home. Domestic violence affects, men, women and children. Compared to battles and wars, many more people are harmed at home. There are literally millions seriously hurt world-wide every day and night. The harm is physical and psychological. There are a high number of deaths every day, and although there are a huge number of people treated for injuries, that is only a tiny proportion of those suffering every single minute which do not get recorded.

There are no figures available to give an indication of how many children are harmed when they see their own parents battered –often one battering the other. Yet despite the massive scale of the harm, there is proportionately little attention given to it. One celebrity scandal, garners far more attention.

This book focuses on two things: One. Persuading politicians to do more with legislation and administrative practices and give people the protection they desperately need. Two. Provide much more co-ordinated and effective help at a Sovereign State level to victims of these appalling crimes. This should not have to rely on public spirited donations. And the message should extend to outside the home too, to parks and streets; to everywhere, in fact.

Politicians argue that this is a cultural and social problem. They are more concerned with budgetary matters and they believe the voters are more concerned with money too. I do not believe voters would be begrudge a couple of dollars a month to render them safer. It is easy to ignore what we do not see and hear and say that it is just one of those things. But the message in respect of the first step is not difficult to take in: Stop hitting us

[Soon, available free in perpetuity.]

TREAD SOFTLY BECAUSE you tread on my dreams
WB Yeats

michaelttwilliams.com

Michael TT Williams

Imagination stretched to the limit

Don't miss out!

Visit the website below and you can sign up to receive emails whenever Michael TT Williams publishes a new book. There's no charge and no obligation.

https://books2read.com/r/B-A-TNHO-TGSPB

www.ingramcontent.com/pod-product-compliance
Lightning Source LLC
Chambersburg PA
CBHW031630170726
47990CB00017B/440